The Rebels of JOURNEY'S End

DIANA FRANCES BELL

PENGUI
by arrangem

D1437638

Penguin Books Ltd, Harmondsworth,
Middlesex, England
Penguin Books Australia Ltd, Ringwood,
Victoria, Australia

First published by Hutchinson 1966
Published in Puffin Books 1969
Copyright © Diana Frances Bell, 1966
Illustrations copyright © Hutchinson & Co.
(Publishers) Ltd, 1966

Made and printed in Great Britain by
Richard Clay (The Chaucer Press) Ltd,
Bungay, Suffolk
Set in Linotype Baskerville

This book is sold subject to the condition that
it shall not, by way of trade or otherwise, be lent,
re-sold, hired out, or otherwise circulated without
the publisher's prior consent in any form of
binding or cover other than that in which it is
published and without a similar condition
including this condition being imposed on the
subsequent purchaser

PUFFIN BOOKS

Editor: Kaye Webb

The Rebels of Journey's End

Rufus Mouse's troubles began one cold, windswept day when he read a notice hanging outside a notorious backstreet mousehole. It said: *'Wanted, mice to work. Good pay. Apply Joe Fingers within.'*

Rufus wasn't at all the kind of mouse you would expect to see working in the headquarters of the mouse underworld, but he and his family had to live, and there was no honest work to be had. Because he had been buying up shops one by one, Joe Fingers had gained control of most of the Mousetown business, and it was very difficult for anyone else to set up in business.

Then Joe Fingers ordered Rufus to kidnap a valuable cat and hold him hostage, and Rufus rebelled at last. With his friends Rikiki the cat, Oscar the chipmunk and a little girl called Donna, he set up an organization called the Rebels of Journey's End.

Diana Frances Bell was only thirteen years old when she wrote this unusual and lively story, so she is the youngest author ever to be published in Puffins and she thoroughly deserves the honour.

For readers of 9 and over.

Cover design by Douglas Hall

Illustrated by Douglas Hall

To Rima and Tiki,
the two Siamese cats who inspired Rikiki

Contents

PART ONE

The Band is Formed

CHAPTER I

The Plight of Rikiki

A pair of round, perfectly blue eyes gazed down, disturbed, at the sight below them. The Siamese cat was sitting on his favourite place of refuge, an old, oaken mantelpiece. There, if he wished, he could strain back behind the flower vase and out of the reach of his mistress.

It had all begun earlier that morning. Miss Spottle, a dignified elderly spinster, had been in a cheerful mood for once. She was tall and thin, with cold, rather short-sighted eyes. She possessed only a limited wardrobe of three dresses. One dark blue, one canary yellow and the other a plum colour. Rikiki (for that was the cat's name) could tell what her temper was by what she wore. Today it was the plum colour. That had warned him from the start what sort of a day it would be, for when Miss Spottle was cheerful it was the first sign of a cat show.

It was not long before his fears were confirmed. He heard the trotting footsteps as his owner mounted the stairs. Her bedroom door squeaked as it opened. He could see in his mind's eye her movements from now on. She would be walking to the dressing table and pulling out the bottom drawer. Kneeling down, she would rummage in it till she found the thing she was seeking, the piece of paper he hated so very, very much. His pedigree.

How he disliked cat shows! Miss Spottle would throw tea parties for the judges and always managed to bring the conversation round to her 'darling Rikiki' and his famous ancestors. Then she would show them his pedigree, and all the while Rikiki would be feigning sleep on a glossy red cushion that he wasn't normally allowed to touch.

He could also expect the biggest insult a cat could ever receive. A bath! Perhaps it was the sound of running water in preparation for this that finally made him decide to run away. He had thought of it often before, but had kept putting it off. He tried desperately to think of a plan of escape. He didn't have long and at first an idea just wouldn't come. Finally, however, he decided. Having done so he waited expectantly for his mistress's call.

'Riki pussy,' he heard her whine at last. 'Come and get some meat. Lots of nice juicy meat for pussums. Here Riki-Riki.'

'Rubbish!' he thought, 'but seeing it's part of my plan, I suppose I do as she says.' So he padded out to the kitchen, and, as he expected, a hand grabbed him by the scruff of the neck.

'Aha!' came a triumphant cry from Miss Spottle, 'got you.' With long strides she made her way to the laundry, where a tub of soapy water awaited the poor cat. He was plunged in and soaped well all over before he managed to gather his wits and remember his plan of escape.

The tub of water he was being bathed in was

directly below a window. And (surely luck was on his side) that window was open! Gathering his strength, Rikiki took a leap on to the broad window-sill. With another that scattered soapsuds in Miss Spottle's horrified face, he leapt into the garden and away across the lawn.

'This is the first time I've been past the fence,' Rikiki thought as he jumped over it. 'Except, of course, for the times they put me in a box for the cat shows.' He shuddered as he thought of it. 'Now I'm free at last. What a strange feeling it is! Wonderful! Why didn't I do it before?'

Rikiki forgot that he had only been free a few minutes. He was happily ignorant as he strolled down the pavement, the warmth of the afternoon sun on his back. He listened to the birds as they sang in the trees above him. He paddled joyfully in the stream of rain-water as it rippled down the gutter. He meowed full-throatedly for the very love of it. The soapsuds had dried stiffly on his back, and though they felt a little queer, nothing could mar his happiness.

He soon reached the shopping centre, where a fox

terrier with a rakish patch on his side was sitting with his back to Rikiki, watching the traffic roll by. Occasionally he would give expressive little barks as a particularly noisy car or motor-cycle passed him.

In a few moments the dog turned and saw him. Rikiki arched instinctively and spat. The terrier gave a howl of rage. He hurled himself at the doorway. But by the time he reached it, the doorway was empty.

As he flew down the footpath, Rikiki told himself that he'd never been so frightened in his life before. He could hear the dog's panting breath at his heels. For a moment he was overcome with terror. But his pace never slackened.

In a little while he felt himself growing tired. But not too tired to think. He was approaching a corner, so he decided to try to shake the dog off. He ran round it, and ducked into the doorway of the nearest shop, praying as hard as he could that the terrier hadn't seen him. Then a few seconds later he heard him round the corner and race on. He was safe.

He didn't know what to do now, so he just sauntered along, looking with interest at the legs that were hurrying past him. When he came to shops that had low windows he found he could gaze inside by standing on his hind legs and placing his front paws on the window-pane. Soon he came to a place that seemed different from the others. He didn't know, but this was a butcher's shop. Intrigued by the smells, he slipped in when a customer opened the door.

It was delightfully cool inside and the sawdust on the floor was soft on his feet. The atmosphere soothed him after the shock he'd just had.

He was to receive yet another shock, however. Out of the blue he felt the straw end of a broom hit roughly across his back. He lost his footing and skidded across the floor. Again and again it happened, and each time he tripped and skidded. And he suddenly realized that he had been swept out of the shop!

He looked up. And he saw a man towering over him. He was taller than anyone he had ever seen before. And he had a tremendous moustache. It wiggled as he mouthed:

'We'll have no strays like you around the place. Off with you and don't you be so bold as to put one foot in my shop again.'

Rikiki fled.

When he slowed down he had to face facts. It was growing dark and he had nowhere to go. He slunk along the pavement, keeping to the shadows for fear someone would see him. He had had enough of humans for one day and he didn't want any more fearsome encounters. He wondered desperately what he was going to do. He was tired. He had long since left the shopping centre and at least his head was not swimming with the noise caused by the departing shoppers. He turned into Journey Street. 'If I don't find anywhere,' he thought, 'then I'll curl up on the nearest doorstep.'

But he did find somewhere; it was an old deserted house. True, from what he could see cobwebs decorated most of the windows and he wasn't very fond of spiders; still, it looked dry enough and he could do much worse.

He lay down, flattened out and squeezed under the

gate through a space that proved to be narrower than he expected. But after wriggles and numerous man-oeuvres to the widest part, he managed to arrive on the other side. He walked rather slowly up what he guessed had once been a path and stared round at the garden. The grass, that might have looked so magnifi-cent as a smooth lawn of green velvet rolling down a slight slope to the fence, was just a patch of browny green, in some parts as high as a human's waist. The trees that grew quite near the house might have been, in days long gone, orderly sentinels trimmed to per-fection. 'Now,' Rikiki reflected, 'they look more like the scraggy bits of bush Miss Spottle sticks in her sand models.'

Then he saw why the house and grounds were in such a state. In the middle of the garden, rising from a patch of rose bushes, was a bit of notice-board. Though it was nearly dark, there was enough twilight to make out what it said. '—R SALE.' He looked at it thought-fully. The words were hardly discernible, so much paint had worn away. Then he shook his head sadly and continued on his way.

When he reached the door he nosed at it timidly. It swung open with an alarming creak. He jumped. Looking round nervously, he crept inside. He found himself in a large hallway, decorated here and there with spider webs and birds' nests. Their owners had found the place dry and warm. But Rikiki saw no-where that he could sleep. At the right of the hallway were some stairs. He decided to mount them and try his luck. When he did so, however, he was nearly frightened out of his wits. He was greeted with a harsh voice asking:

'What's the password?'

Rikiki was face to face with a huge black spider suspended in space above the fifth stair.

'I don't know,' he stammered.

The spider looked at him queerly. What on earth was this animal doing here if he didn't know the password? After a few minutes' deep thinking he decided on a course of action. 'That'll do,' he replied. 'Those who don't know it are permitted to travel through if they say that.' With a wave of one of his hairy legs he added, 'Continue.'

Rikiki did so. He found some nice comfortable straw in the room opposite the top of the stairs. It was lovely and soft. He had nearly dozed off when suddenly he felt hungry. Terribly hungry. He hadn't eaten since the day before. It had been almost feeding time when he had run away. But he was too sleepy now to get anything. Get anything! He sat up on the straw in fright. How was he going to eat now? Then he told himself sternly:

'You're an alley cat now, so you do what the alley cats do.' And he settled down in the gloom of the old house and drifted into miserable sleep.

The Plight of Rufus

On a cold, windswept day, three months before Rikiki's escape, the story of Rufus had begun. A notice had been hanging outside one of the notorious back-street mouseholes. It had said: *'Wanted, mice to work. Good pay. Apply Joe Fingers within'*, and, while stamping his frozen feet, Rufus had read it.

He was a small, plump mouse. He wore spectacles that were inclined to give him a serious look and in spite of his ragged clothes there was an air of respectability about him. In fact he was not at all the sort of mouse that one would expect to be standing outside the headquarters of the mouse underworld.

But, like so many others, he had a reason. Like so many others Rufus had to swallow his pride and beg a job from Joe Fingers. For, although this hurt him deeply, he and his family had to live.

It had happened very slowly. So slowly that Mouse-town had hardly been aware that anything out of the ordinary was going on before, one by one, they had fallen under the tyranny of the head of the underworld and his associates. It had begun with the shops. Gradually, by buying up a shop here and a chain of stores there, 'the Boss', as the head mouse became known, soon controlled most of the Mousetown business. If a mouse with little money tried to set up an honest trade of his own, he was always beaten by the underworld organization. There were a few who had enough money and influence to stand up against the monopoly, but these were so few that the Boss didn't bother about them, and, indeed, he had little need to.

Rufus was the eldest son of the mice who lived in Buttercup Field. He had eleven small brothers and sisters to support. Mr and Mrs Whiskers did their best, but the small wage that Mr Whiskers earned as a mill assistant did little towards the upkeep of the family. So, now that he was old enough to work, the brunt of the burden fell upon Rufus and, as jobs were so scarce, all he could do was to join the organization.

The roaring and shouting of many mice greeted his ears as he plucked up courage and walked into the mousehole. There seemed to be some sort of contest going on. He stood on the edge of the crowd of workers and watched. A rope was strung across from one rafter to another (mouseholes usually had rafters to strengthen the ceilings) and on that rope balanced two mice. He had never seen anything like it before in his life.

'What's happening?' he ventured to ask timidly of a rather bored-looking mouse standing next to him.

The mouse turned and glared fiercely at him. 'The Boss is defending his title, of course, stupid.'

Rufus didn't like to ask what title that was, as the mouse had turned his back. He concluded, however, that the balancing must be some sort of sport in the underworld. He guessed, quite rightly, that no one would be interested in his inquiry for a job at the moment, so he stood still and went on watching.

Suddenly one of the mice wobbled and fell. There was a great cheering as the mouse still on the rope held up his fat arm. A loud voice proclaimed, 'Once again, the Boss is the winner.'

It was then that Rufus met the Boss for the first time. He was sitting on a small stool, a gaudily patterned towel slung over his fat shoulders. All his workers and friends (there was a distinct difference; his workers hated him and his ideas but had to pretend otherwise to get paid; his friends hated him also, but then they approved of his ideas) surrounded him, full of praise. A large cigar hung from his mouth and, as Rufus struggled through the crowd, the first indication that he was reaching his goal was the fact that the smoke was growing thicker and thicker.

Before he realized it, he was out of the mice and in front of the Boss. He was looked up and down. 'What do you want?' asked the leader of the underworld in his oily voice.

'A job please, sir,' Rufus answered politely.

The Boss looked amused. 'Well, if you're willing to do the work – say,' he beckoned to the bored-looking mouse Rufus had first spoken to, 'Charlie, over here a minute. Look after this new boy, will you?'

Charlie led him off, deposited him in a dark corner and promptly forgot him. Thus Rufus became one of the many thousands who worked for the terrible Joe Fingers.

*

The day he was appointed second-in-command was the time his troubles really began. A little more than three months had passed since he joined up, and he was the envy of every mouse in the organization. For some unfathomable reason, even to Rufus himself, the Boss had taken a liking to the shy little mouse. He had risen from tenth in command to third in command. Now, when the words 'Send Rufus in' echoed over the intercom, everyone was pretty sure why he had been sent for.

And they were right. When he walked into the most luxurious of all the backstreet mouseholes the Boss didn't beat about the bush. He told Rufus straight away that he was giving him more power than any other mouse in the business except himself.

Rufus sat down unsteadily in the chair opposite the Boss. 'Why me?' he squeaked in amazement. 'Why not one of the others?'

The Boss reached for a cigar. He lit it in deep thought. Smoke curled to the ceiling as he held it in his plump paw. Suddenly, after minutes of silence, he spoke. 'I don't really know, Rufus. Perhaps because everyone else is too ambitious to take my place. Perhaps because you are different, quieter and consequently more trustworthy. Do you see?'

'I think so,' the mouse replied, 'but I don't want to accept. I wouldn't be any good really – '

He didn't get any farther. A dangerous glint crept into the Boss's eyes. 'You will do as I say and we will speak no more about it.'

Rufus shifted uncomfortably on his chair. He hated his work. In fact he hated anything to do with the underworld. He was horrified at the idea that he was becoming one of its leaders. Every time he had been promoted he had protested. But it was no use. The Boss's word was final, and the Boss had made up his mind.

'Well, that's settled.' The Boss blew a ring of smoke into the air. 'Now I have some very important things to tell you. Firstly, I'm going to let you into my biggest secret. This is one you must promise not to reveal until I have announced it.'

Rufus nodded his head.

'I am going to declare war on the cats.'

Rufus nearly fell out of his chair. 'The cats!' he exclaimed, hoping that he hadn't heard correctly.

'Ssh,' ordered the Boss, looking round nervously. 'Yes. Now let me explain before you start protesting. Your first mission as my second-in-command will spark it off. You are going to kidnap a very valuable cat and hold him as hostage. This will make the cats extremely angry; and there – you have it.'

'The war?'

'Exactly. The cats will not tolerate such audacity from us mice. They think us very weak. But I am working on something that will proclaim us superior once and for all.'

Rufus was horrified. So these were the evil things that were going on in the Boss's mind.

'Now, more about your mission,' the Boss went on. 'I shall give you, let me see, yes, a squad of about a hundred mice should do, and you will go to this address.' He pushed a piece of paper under Rufus's nose.

No. 50 Journey Street, it read.

'What will I do there?' he asked apprehensively.

'When you arrive you will find our spy waiting for you. His name is Black Jake. He is a very large spider and you will easily recognize him. He will give you the cat if you give him the password.'

Rufus scratched his nose nervously. It all sounded so organized. 'What are you going to do with this cat when he's captured, sir?' he asked.

'Don't call me sir, Rufus. Now that you're my right-hand mouse, I think you could call me Joe.'

To Rufus the very fact that the Boss avoided answering his question boded ill for the cat. 'Yes, sir – er – Joe,' he replied.

'Now – ' began the Boss.

Rufus interrupted. 'I suppose I HAVE to go on this mission?'

'You do.'

'Please, Joe, I'd be sure to bungle it. I'm really a most incompetent mouse,' he pleaded.

'Nonsense, Rufus. I have a lot of faith in you, my boy. You'd better be running along now, we've had quite a long conversation. And remember, all my plans are the deadliest secrets. Not a word to the boys out there, though they're sure to be curious.'

Rufus stood up. He was just about to go when he thought of something. 'Oh, Joe, you haven't told me when I'm going to do this mission.'

The Boss had finished his cigar. He pulled another from his top drawer. 'Tomorrow,' he answered. 'To-morrow morning at nine. I'll have the mice ready here, and then you can march into Journey Street.'

Rufus was thunderstruck. So soon! He had counted on another week. He tried to think of an excuse to put it off, but the only words that came to his lips were: 'Are you sure the cat will still be there?'

'Quite sure. See you tomorrow.'

Rufus felt weak at the knees. He opened the door and escaped out of the smoky room. Seeing the mice inspecting him, he pretended to cough.

'Well, Rufus, what did the Boss want you for, eh?' began Charlie.

Rufus fixed him with a rather frightened look and said, 'The Boss just appointed me second-in-command,' and disappeared outside.

As he strolled along the dark, deserted streets, he wondered what the next day would be like. He'd been on missions before, but none as bad as this promised to be. If only there wasn't such a need for him to work with the underworld, and if he thought he could possibly get away with it he would have tried to get out, and set up an honest business of his own. But he'd seen others try it, and they weren't alive to tell the tale. If only he had known, really known, what it was like when he first joined. Once you were in the organization, you were in it for keeps.

At last he was away from the backstreet area and Buttercup Field was in sight. He walked along the worn footpath and watched as the stars came out, one by one. Then he reached the field and felt the velvety touch of the flowers as they brushed his back.

'Be there at nine,' Rufus whispered aloud. 'I will have to, I suppose.' And he walked up the winding path to his door.

CHAPTER 3

Rufus Makes a Decision

A small stream cut its way through the buttercups and rippled by not far from Rufus's window. As the first rays of dawn peeped over the horizon next morning the mouse rose and went down to the water's edge, just where a huge fern grew at a bend in the stream.

He had tossed and turned all night. How he wished he didn't have to obey the Boss! He had thought and thought, trying to find a way for him to get out of it so that his family would not be hurt. As far as he could see there was no hope – unless a miracle happened, and miracles were not likely to happen to a poor mouse like him.

The fern frond swayed above him. A small breeze had sprung up from nowhere. The sun was up now, and shining gladly down on everything. Rufus realized that he had better be getting home or his family would start worrying.

Coming back over the huge stones and through the forest of yellow flowers, he found himself perched for a moment on a gigantic rock. Looking down, he saw the postman treading wearily towards their home. Rufus wondered what was in the big white envelope he carried under his arm.

❉

When the postman knocked on their door Rufus was already home. The whole family was sitting round the table having breakfast. Jack Whiskers was told to let the old mouse in.

'Mail, special delivery for Mrs Whiskers,' Mr Broadtail informed them.

'Special delivery for me!' Mrs Whiskers exclaimed in astonishment. It was very seldom anything happened to her that was so exciting.

'Yep.' The old postman lifted his cap. 'You'll have to sign for it. Right here on this line, Mrs Whiskers.'

She hurried forward and seized the pen he offered her with trembling hands.

When she received the envelope and opened it, all her children clamoured round crying: 'What is it? What is it, Mum?' But Mrs Whiskers could not answer them. She had fainted.

When she came to on the sofa she gasped, 'Look at the letter,' and handed them a piece of paper.

It read:

J. Flicktail and Flicktail
Solicitors
Winga Wanga

Dear Mrs Whiskers,

It is with sincere regret that I inform you of your great-uncle's death on the fourteenth of September. You will be comforted to know that he passed away peacefully. He left you a sum of money in his will. The will I have enclosed in this letter. The money will be forwarded according to his last instructions.

Yours sincerely,
J. Flicktail Snr

'Oh!' they all gasped.

Mr Whiskers picked up the will, which had fallen to the floor. He unfolded it and began to read. The others waited impatiently as a long list of relations received small sums of money. Then came the last and, to them, the most important paragraph.

This said:

I leave to my dear grand-niece, whom I happen to know has fallen upon hard times, the amount of two thousand pounds, in hopes that this will make her happy.

Jonas Twitch

'Hurray!' shouted Licky Whiskers. They all laughed. Licky was the youngest of the clan and hardly able to talk; he couldn't have understood very much of the will. When he saw everyone's happy face, however, he had expressed their feelings with the newest word in his vocabulary.

The mousehole became a scene of frantic joy and gaiety. None of them except Mrs Whiskers had known their benefactor, so they could hardly be expected to mourn him.

There was one other mousehole in Buttercup Field besides that of the Whiskers family. It belonged to the Longnoses. Mr Longnose was one of the few who were able, because of their wealth and power, to stand up to the Boss and run grocery shops of their own.

Mr Longnose had been sleeping in. Now, however – he was awake, and mad! The noise that the joyful Whiskers family had been making wafted through to his room. He put on his dressing gown, explained to his wife, who insisted on coming with him to see what it was all about, and raced out to pound on his neighbour's door.

'Open up, you sleepwreckers!' he demanded angrily.

When the door was opened at last they were confronted with Mrs Whiskers' face so full of happiness that they gasped. 'Do come in and join the fun, Mr and Mrs Longnose,' she said. 'Something wonderful has happened to us.'

So they went in, full of curiosity.

They were almost as pleased as their neighbours when they heard of the inheritance. They all sat round in the living room drinking tiny cups of coffee and discussed seriously what was to be done with the two thousand pounds. The Longnoses were very good at suggestions, as they were quite well off themselves.

'Of course, you'll have to have the mousehole on the other side of us; it's in a much better position and less likely to be flooded. You're too near the Buttercup stream here.'

'Yes,' said Mrs Whiskers thoughtfully, 'and all of us must have new clothes.' She looked sadly at the rags her children were wearing. 'All the night I've spent trying to make Rufus's old clothes do for Jack, and Jack's do for someone else. By the time they reach Licky they're so full of darns and patches that they have to be thrown away.'

Mr Whiskers looked about their home. 'And at last we can have some proper furniture,' he added.

Mrs Whiskers turned joyfully to her eldest son. 'And now poor Rufus won't have to work for that horrible what's-his-name Fingers.'

Rufus opened his mouth to say something, then

closed it again. How could he explain that it was just not possible? It was not as if he was only one of the nameless mice, who might have had a chance of slipping away unnoticed. Now it was all even more terrible than it had been before. Yesterday he had had a reason for being in the employ of Joe Fingers. Now he had not.

'My goodness!' he suddenly exclaimed. 'What's the time?'

'A quarter to – oh, my dear boy – nine!' replied his father in a fluster. 'You'd better run all the way to work if you don't want to be late.'

It was then that Rufus made up his mind. He just could not obey the Boss's order. He just could not. If he didn't he and his family would most probably die. But he had an answer to that problem now. He dashed

out of the living room into the hall. 'If I can only make them understand,' he thought, 'if they will do as I say, then they might have a chance.' He reached his bedroom. He found a piece of paper and began to write, sitting at his earthy desk.

My dear, dear family,

You will be surprised at receiving a note from me, but I have several very important things to tell you. I could not have done so earlier without spoiling your happiness, so I am doing it now. Firstly, I had better correct your ideas about my job. I am second-in-command and I could not, under any circumstances, just 'leave' and not expect any consequences.

My Boss is an evil mouse. From the time you get this note you must follow my instructions carefully. You see, I am about to do something that will make him very angry. He will want to get his revenge.

None of you must venture on to the streets alone from now on. Pack all your belongings and go to the underground railway. Catch the first train to Cornfield Village where you will be safe. Settle there and on no account move until you next hear from me.

I am going on a mission today, the most terrible the Boss has yet made me do. But I am determined about one thing. Although I intend to turn up for it, somehow, whatever else I have to do, I AM NOT GOING THROUGH WITH IT.

> That I swear.
> All my most precious love,
> Rufus

*

He wound his way through the buttercups and clover, twisting along the countless ways and short cuts to the footpath. It took longer than usual, for he was not concentrating and every now and again he would wander on to the wrong track. But he reached it at last and sat down on a stone to catch his breath.

He looked at his mouse-size watch. Ten past nine. He was late. They would be waiting for him now, amazed that he wasn't punctual. No one but the Boss was ever late. He didn't care. Even if he had he couldn't have done anything about it, for there was a good five minutes' more walking to his destination. So when he stood up again he took it casually, trotting at his own steady pace.

As he went along he was forming his plan. It had first come to him when he made his decision. He thought it over, improved on it. It had to be carried out very cleverly to work, and Rufus hoped with all his heart that he could do it properly.

He was almost there now. It was twenty past nine. He guessed that the mice were not very pleased with him. He was right. He could hear a loud, impatient murmuring as he approached the offices. He descended the steps to the smoke-filled mousehole. The sea of waiting faces swam before his eyes. He wondered where the Boss was. He choked for a moment on the smoke. There were a few angry shouts from the crowd as they got over the momentary shock of seeing him. With fear in his heart, Rufus realized it was time to put his plan into action.

CHAPTER 4

Escape

Rikiki had woken early on the morning after his arrival. He was just in time to see the dawn chase away the dark. He had sat up rather weakly and abruptly sneezed. His first thought was to get away from this horrible dusty old house, where spiders demanded passwords and cobwebs hung from your ears when you woke up. But he soon found he could not. The door was locked.

He banged at it. He even went as far as standing on his hind legs and trying to reach the doorknob. It was all in vain. He sat down and yowled mournfully for someone to come and let him out. But no one came. There was no Miss Spottle to open the door, pick him up and soothe him in her sugary (sickening, but at least he had been taken notice of) voice. He yowled again in vain, and when at last he saw it was no use he wandered sadly back to the straw he had slept on. He looked around, for he had been too tired the night before to take much in. There was nothing really of interest except a few old packing cases in a corner.

Rikiki suddenly realized how hungry he was. He had eaten nothing since yesterday. Sniffing round the packing cases, he found some bits of bread that a tramp must have left there while sheltering in the old house.

Not that the cat liked bread very much, but there was nothing else and it didn't seem too stale.

He chewed the bread slowly and wondered whether he had done the right thing in leaving Miss Spottle. Rikiki licked the last crumb from his coat and went back to sleep on the straw, still hungry and now a little worried.

*

Rufus drew himself up and fixed as cold a stare as he could manage upon the nearest mouse in the room, who happened to be Charlie. 'Will you kindly inform the Boss that I am here?' he ordered.

You could have heard a pin drop in the astonished quiet that followed. Rufus had never been known to give an order before in his life.

Charlie gasped. For a moment he had been about to say 'Go tell him yourself,' when he caught a new look in Rufus's eyes, commanding and icy.

'Well, didn't you hear me?' thundered Rufus. 'Go and tell him I have arrived.' He was rather enjoying himself now, though he had been petrified at first. He had been rather frightened that Charlie wouldn't obey him, but the mouse scampered off and he heaved a sigh of relief. So far his desperate scheme was working.

Suddenly a voice cut like a whiplash across the room. The Boss was standing in the doorway of his office.

'Well, well. So his lordship has decided to join us at last. May I ask where you have been?'

Rufus froze. All his assurance melted away from him at the first words of his employer. He couldn't speak for a moment; he was terrified. But at last he found his voice and squeaked:

'I was delayed.' Then to his relief he felt his confidence flow back and he added, 'But better late than never, eh, Joe?'

The mice gasped for the second time. Rufus had dared to call the Boss by his first name! Horror of horrors, what would he do to him?

The Boss put his head on one side and considered. This was the last answer he had expected from Rufus. Even if he had given him permission to call him Joe, there was no need to show off about it. Still, it was too late now, and there was no point in revealing his annoyance until later.

'Yes indeed, Rufus,' he agreed, speaking after what seemed an age of silence, 'but you had better hurry now. Black Jake might be having trouble holding the cat.'

The mice could hardly believe their ears.

'Everybody into line,' ordered the Boss, 'and remember to keep in order because you'll probably have a lot of mice watching you.'

So they all set off. The Boss, who of course was not going, farewelled them from the entrance of the headquarters. Rufus felt scared and self-conscious as he marched at the head of the long line. They were really on their way there now. Each mouse was armed with a needle dagger and together they carried a huge sheet in which they hoped to entrap the cat. They looked a ferocious lot as they stamped relentlessly past the hundreds of mouse spectators that lined the footpaths.

At length they passed out of the backstreet area,

which meant there would be no more watchers. They
were relieved. At intervals they stopped and rested.
But not for long. On and on they tramped and at
length they filed down Journey Street. Finally they
stopped outside the old house that stood at the very
end. The dead end. On the gatepost was the number
50.

Rikiki was woken by the sounds of shouts and grim
laughter in the garden below. He rose and looked out
of the window. The sight of a squad of mice brandish-

ing needle daggers met his eyes. What on earth was
happening?

Puffing up the garden path ahead of the others,
Rufus happened to look up. He saw Rikiki on the
window-sill. So this was the cat he had been sent to
capture! He was certainly very handsome. The way he
held up his head; the creaminess of the fur on his back
and the pure chocolate colouring of his muzzle, paws
and tail; the expensive look of his pure leather collar:
they all said he was no ordinary cat.

Rufus knew it was time for the main part of his plan. He climbed with difficulty on to a nearby human-size oil can and held up his arms for silence. Immediately there was silence, for the mice were in awe of this new, capable leader. Rufus said:

'We must decide what we will do.' (He shouted as loud as he could so that Rikiki, watching fascinated, could hear. His plan was first of all to warn the cat somehow. This was the perfect time, as none of the others had spotted him at the window.) 'The cat must be captured skilfully. This is what we will do. All of you will remain here while I talk to the spy who is' (he raised his voice still louder) 'a black spider. Then I will talk to this cat by myself and persuade him to come out peacefully. Right?'

'Right,' chorused the squad rather reluctantly.

Rikiki was taking all this in, horrified, yet extremely puzzled. The little round mouse had obviously seen him, and now he was telling him all the plans! Something very queer was going on. But he had no time to be thinking, they had come here to capture him. He had to find somewhere to hide. Quickly!

Rufus saw the spy as soon as he walked into the house.

'Password?' inquired the spider gruffly.

The mouse replied promptly with the correct word, then said, 'Now, spider, lead me to the prisoner.'

The spider looked at him in surprise. He had heard that the mouse leading the squad was the meekest, most retiring worker in the organization. His information must have been incorrect. This mouse certainly did not fill that description. To be sure he looked the part, but he wasn't acting it. He led him down the hall, up the stairs and indicated the room.

'I heard what you said outside,' he whispered hoarsely, 'so I guess you'll be wanting to see him alone. Well, that's the door,' and having said his piece the spider slid silently away.

Rufus felt sick inside. His teeth were chattering.

What if the cat didn't give him a chance to explain? What if he just pounced and killed him? Well, he'd have to take the chance now, he'd gone too far to back out.

He pushed the door open a little way to see if he could discover where in the room the cat was. But he could not. So, holding his breath, he gave it a hard push. The door opened wide. But there was no sign of Rikiki. The room seemed deserted.

This was something he had not bargained for. Perhaps, however, it was for the better. He knew the cat must be somewhere in the room, so he decided to speak up anyway.

'I know you must be here,' he began, 'and I want you to be kind enough to hear me out. My name is Rufus Whiskers. Until recently I was working for the underworld. Now I am not. Please listen to why and you may understand.'

He explained. And as Rikiki listened to the little grey mouse talking earnestly to someone he couldn't even see he felt strangely inclined to believe him.

When Rufus had finished, and was looking nervously around, he suddenly asked a question. 'Is that why you warned me when you were talking outside the window?'

'Yes,' replied the mouse meekly.

Rikiki thought of something else. 'How do I know you're not just a clever spy who has every intention of betraying me to the Boss?'

Rufus looked distressed. 'Oh dear, I'm afraid I can't prove I'm not. I assure you, though, there is as much danger in this for me as for you. I couldn't stand working for the Boss any more, especially now that he's thought of this terrible plan.'

'It is indeed a terrible plan,' agreed Rikiki.

'Then you'll help me?'

'If you help me.'

'Oh, thank you,' gasped Rufus, 'you don't know what this means to me!'

'Well, I would like to remain alive as long as possible, too, you know.'

Rufus smiled. Rikiki came out from behind the packing cases, introduced himself, and shook hands with his tiny partner. They were friends.

And what a combination they made! Between them they had the bewildered spy and anxious squad of mice running round in circles, trying to obey the most ridiculous orders that Rufus insisted were most essential to the successful capture of the Siamese cat. He told Charlie to go to the nearest mouse-grocer and purchase one hundred and fifty olives. Others he told to buy: two cans of oil, five pounds of mothballs, twenty of the ripest tomatoes they could find and a can of pepper. (All this food was mouse-size; for the mice, as do all the smaller animals who are not domesticated or dependent for survival upon the generosity of humans live in a tiny 'shadow' world all around the humans who have no idea of the extent of its organization. In the case of the mice, everything they eat is grown on mouse-size farms, and everything they use is made in mouse-size factories.) He told the mice to place them all in a pile at the top of the stairs. Rikiki helped in the cause by uttering fierce yowls now and again, so that they echoed gruesomely all over the house.

When finally everything was done, the mice huddled at the foot of the stairs, quite terrified. How brave they thought Rufus when he climbed the stairs and went into the room to talk to the cat!

Rikiki greeted Rufus with twinkling eyes. 'What on earth are we going to do now?' he asked.

As Rufus explained the last part of his plan, something caught Rikiki's eye. He stopped Rufus and pointed to the wall. Then he marched over to it and pulled at a small lever he had noticed beside the window-sill. There was a grinding noise. Part of the wall slid away to reveal a hole.

'A laundry chute!' they exclaimed together.

A laundry chute it was. Rufus had been going to try to escape by way of the window. Down the drain-pipe. He had been fairly sure they wouldn't make it. Now, however, they had a much better chance.

'Hurray!' they cried softly. They peered down. It seemed the very thing.

They had something to do before they could go. They crept out behind the pile of objects at the top of the stairs. Rikiki bent his back to them. He sent them rolling, crashing, slithering and pouring down the stairs. Quickly they hurried back and climbed into the chute. While they slid merrily down, the mice were coated with oil, rubbed with olives and ripe tomatoes, then stuck all over with evil-smelling moth-balls. They looked a sight as they trudged wearily back to report the outrageous episode to their Boss.

CHAPTER 5

Enter Donna

It was only after they had arrived in what seemed to be a cellar that the two conspirators permitted themselves to dissolve in the laughter they had been suppressing.

'What a joke!' chortled Rufus, rolling on the cellar floor in glee.

'Did you see that one trying to get out of the oily mothballs?' cried Rikiki. 'He'll never have the oil off his fur in a month of Sundays.'

'What about the one trapped under the tomato-soup can – I wonder if he ever got out? Oh dear! Oh dear! It was all so funny, I can't stop laughing.'

But of course he did and so did Rikiki, and they settled down on an old mildewed couch to talk of more serious things.

'Well, what will we do now?' Rufus asked. 'They'll be back, we can be sure of that.'

'I don't know. Perhaps if we think a little we might get some kind of an idea.'

They thought.

It wasn't long before Rikiki's eyes gleamed.

'What is it, Rikiki?' Rufus looked at him.

'I want to consider it more before I tell you, Rufus, because it would have to be done terribly well for the Boss to be taken in by it.'

'Oh,' said Rufus, a little hurt, 'well, we had better decide where we're going to hide out. The Boss is very clever at finding escapers. I've seen how he does it.'

Rikiki looked thoughtful. 'That's where you're going to be very useful. You know all his methods, don't you?' he said.

'Yes, I do, and most of the spies, too.'

Rikiki looked round him. The cellar was dark and very dusty. It had once been used as a laundry for there were two big tubs in the corner. Various crates and the old couch were the only other furniture. It had two entrances. One was the chute. The other was a trapdoor at the top of a flight of stone steps that led to the outside.

'Why don't we make this our hideout?' the cat asked.

Rufus looked round too. 'Why, yes,' he agreed at last, 'this is the perfect place.'

So they set energetically to work to clean it up. They fashioned a tiny broom from some straw and a piece of stick and Rufus ran about sweeping till the air was thick with dust. 'Rufus!' Rikiki choked, 'stop that! Let the dust settle and sweep gently!'

'Yes, sir!' obeyed Rufus, saluting, and Rikiki had to smile.

Rikiki filled a jar of water at the tubs and sloshed it over the floor. Taking turns at a broken old scrubbing brush, they cleaned the floor with a will. Then they chopped up the old crates, and Rikiki, discovering that he had rather a talent for carpentering, made some queerly shaped but none the less sturdy furniture.

Then there was the problem of where to sleep. They

decided at last that the cat would make himself a bed out of a crate and Rufus would sleep beside him in a sardine can they had found empty.

There was no difficulty about food. Stored away in the crates were some goods which humans must have put away and forgotten some time ago; and because these things were human-size, they would keep the animals going for quite a while. The food included such things as: three tins of Romanoff's finest meat-balls in tomato sauce, a large can of salmon and, to Rikiki's extreme delight, about fifteen full sardine cans. There was a whole case of assorted canned food (plus can opener) and another case of extremely mouldy vegetables unfortunately far too old to eat. Altogether these stores would keep them provided for almost as long as they cared to stay.

'Isn't this wonderful?' sighed Rikiki, lying back on his bed when all their efforts had resulted in making a comfortable home.

'It is indeed.' Rufus took off his glasses and rubbed his tired eyes.

'This is better than anything I ever did at Miss Spottle's,' Rikiki said dreamily. 'Oh, the horrible things I used to suffer there, Rufus.'

'I had a good home,' the mouse's voice was sad, 'but it was better for them that I left.'

Then there was a long but friendly silence as each remembered his past.

*

They had been living in their new home about three days when it happened. Rufus had begged Rikiki several times to tell him what his idea was, but he had insisted that the time had not yet come. The thing that occurred, however, was soon to change his mind.

They woke up at three o'clock one morning when there was a loud crash somewhere above them.

Rikiki sat up warily in bed. Rufus pushed his nose over the rim of his sardine can. 'What was that?' they asked together in frightened tones.

'Perhaps someone left a window open and the wind blew something over,' Rikiki suggested.

'But,' Rufus began, 'there is no one to leave a window open except us and we haven't been upstairs at all.'

Rikiki looked at him queerly. 'That's a point,' he agreed reluctantly, 'then it couldn't have been that.'

'Do – do you suppose that there's someone up there then?' Rufus suggested nervously.

'Well,' said Rikiki, fastening his collar round his neck, 'there's only one way to find out.'

'Wait!' Rufus cried after the disappearing figure. 'I'll come too.'

They made their way together up the dark laundry chute (this it was possible to do as there were plenty of footholds where the sides had worn away). Rikiki, being a cat, was able to see in the dark so he gathered up his friend, perched him on top of his head, and continued upwards, using his eyes for both of them. When they reached the top they looked cautiously around, trying to decide where the noise had come from.

Then they heard the sobs. Rikiki stiffened.

'Ah, I think it's coming from that room near the end

of the passage,' said Rufus, relatively unconcerned. They crept past the top of the stairs quietly. The sobs grew slightly louder.

As they moved stealthily along the second-storey hall, Rikiki's footsteps began to falter. He stopped unexpectedly and Rufus, walking behind, bumped into him.

'Sorry, Rufus,' apologized Rikiki, picking up his little companion, 'but I've been thinking. This could easily be dangerous.'

'Oh?'

'Well, what I meant was that perhaps we'd better not . . .'

'Better not investigate? Rikiki!'

Rikiki looked defiantly at him. 'It might be a trap or – or something.'

'That isn't the way the Boss does things. You're just a coward, Rikiki.'

That was more than Rikiki could take.

'Come on,' he said gruffly, pulling Rufus with him, 'or we'll be too late.'

They arrived outside the room. Whoever it was was still crying.

The door was ajar. They pushed it open.

A girl of about ten or eleven years old was kneeling in the middle of the floor trying to pick up the pieces of a broken vase. (It was one the land agent had put lilies in to brighten up the room.) She had long tight plaits and dark brown eyes. She was wearing a faded blue dress and a white cardigan too small for her. She looked grubby, tired, tearful, yet very sweet. She looked up terrified as the door creaked.

'Don't be frightened, we won't hurt you,' assured Rufus before he knew what he was doing.

The girl looked astonished. 'Why, you spoke!' she exclaimed.

'Rufus!' cried Rikiki in a very shocked voice, 'now you've broken the code!'

Rufus hung his head. He looked very miserable. 'I didn't mean to, truly I didn't. It's just that she looked so scared.' He looked up and saw Rikiki's stern face. 'Oh, I know that isn't any excuse, but –'

'The only thing we can do now,' broke in Rikiki, 'is to make her take the promise.'

The girl looked puzzled. 'What's all this about?' she asked.

'I'm sorry,' Rikiki said, 'you don't know about it, do you? Well, now that you've discovered the secret you might as well know the rest. Every animal in the world

that has come in contact with man can speak. That is, he can speak whatever language that man speaks. Take, for example, say, a cat that lives in France will speak French. Do you see?'

'Yes, but why don't they, and what is this code you mentioned?'

'Well, the reason we don't is that humans, from the beginning of time, have treated animals as inferiors. Well, one day three dogs got tired of this so they took the trouble to learn the language. Do you know what happened to them? They were laughed at and sacrificed to the gods. So from that day on the animals swore never to speak again to humans. Our ancestors devised the "Code of Speaking Laws" and they have been handed down through the centuries to us.'

'What are they?' asked the girl curiously.

'We might as well tell her,' said Rufus, 'she knows so much already.'

'All right,' agreed Rikiki.

The two animals said it together.

'The Code of Animal-speaking Laws

1. No animal of any race who is familiar with any human language must speak it within hearing of any person.

2. The only time the language may be spoken is when an animal is conversing with another animal out of the hearing of a human.

3. If it is impossible to avoid speaking to a human for some urgent reason, then this person must promise in writing never to reveal the taking place of such a conversation.

The End'

'So you see now what I meant when I said you would have to take the promise, don't you?' Rikiki inquired.

'Oh yes, and I will gladly if you want me to.'

'What's your name?' asked Rikiki, 'and what are you doing here?'

'My name is Donna Leyland and the reason I'm here is a very long story.'

'If you'd rather not tell us . . .' began Rufus.

'Oh, I don't mind, you've been so kind to me, but perhaps I had better take the promise first to get it over,' she replied.

'Of course. Would you like to come down to our little home in the cellar to do it?'

'I'd love to,' Donna said warmly.

So they marched together down along the passage in the gloomy light of early morning. 'This is fun,' Donna whispered to Rikiki.

Suddenly Rufus stopped dead in his tracks. 'Rikiki, I've just thought of something,' he exclaimed. 'Donna won't be able to fit down our chute!'

'Oh no!' Rikiki said despairingly, 'neither she will.'

Donna looked from one to the other. Tears of exhaustion and disappointment glistened in her eyes. 'You mean I won't be able to come now?'

Rikiki hated to see her cry. 'If only there were some other way,' he began. He snapped his fingers. 'Of course! I noticed before that there's another way into the cellar – a trapdoor leading in from the garden.'

So they crept downstairs. Rikiki expected that there would be a great mess at the foot of them, from their escapade a few days ago. But to his astonishment, except for a large peanut-oil stain and a few mothballs there was nothing. But Rufus was not surprised.

'No doubt the ants had a great feast,' he laughed, 'especially as it was at the Boss's expense.'

They went out the front door. The moon was full and cast so much light that it was quite easy to find the cellar trapdoor. The bolt on it looked old and rusty. Donna viewed it doubtfully. 'It's old, but probably strong. I hope it isn't stuck.' She tugged at it. It didn't budge an inch, but the door swung backwards, after a lot of persuading, with a loud creak that hung on the air long after it had stopped.

'How lovely!' gasped Donna when she saw their hideaway.

'It is rather,' agreed the two animals proudly.

They went down the flight of stone stairs and into the cellar. Donna sat down on a packing-case chair that Rikiki indicated. He fetched a piece of paper. 'Just to say that you heard an animal speak and that now you know about the code of speaking laws you are promising not to tell anyone about them.'

She obeyed him and after signing it handed it to him to look over. 'Very good,' he said, and put it away in a drawer. 'Now would you like something to eat? You look hungry.'

'Yes, I would, please, I haven't eaten since yesterday.'

There was a short pause in the conversation during which only the rattle of cans as Rufus prepared the meal could be heard. Donna opened her mouth to say something, then closed it again.

Plucking up courage she said, 'I'll tell you why I'm here now while you're busy, if that's all right.'

Rikiki and Rufus had their backs to her. They didn't turn round, guessing that she was a little nervous. 'Sure,' Rikiki said.

Donna began, and they all listened intently.

She told them that when her parents had been killed in a car crash she had been rescued and taken to hospital where she had stayed for some weeks. When she was better the nurses had asked her if she had any relations, but Donna had said that she couldn't think of any.

'Phew!' whistled Rikiki. 'I'd never have to do that. You should see the relations on my pedigree.'

'Well,' Donna continued, 'they wanted to send me to an orphanage, so one night I ran away from the hospital because they were only keeping me there until they found somewhere else for me. Then I saw this old house with no one living in it and thought it would be a good place to sleep. I knocked over the vase in the dark and was picking up the pieces and crying when you came in.'

'What a story!' breathed Rikiki, serving her meatballs in a sardine can. Then he pulled Rufus to one side and spoke softly to him. 'Rufus, if we could persuade her to stay, she would be able to help with my plan. All I need is another person for it.'

Rufus eagerly said, 'Oh, do let's try, she's a sweet girl.'

Rikiki solemnly approached Donna and asked: 'We've been thinking. We wondered if you would like to stay here with us?'

Donna smiled delightedly. 'Oh, do you think I might?'

'Of course,' said Rikiki kindly. 'We'd be glad to have you.'

CHAPTER 6

The Spy

When the sun rose on the old bespidered house the next morning it found that two animals and a ten-year-old girl had beaten him to it. Although the animals had been up at three o'clock, they had been sleeping soundly before that, and Donna had been curled up in a corner the day before. In consequence they were not tired and were already up and preparing breakfast.

'Will cocoa and beans be all right?' asked Rufus. It had been agreed that he, having a liking for that sort of thing, should prepare the meals. He found Donna a great help, though, because she was able to use the can opener the animals found too unwieldy to operate.

'Of course,' the other two replied. So after a few moments they were all sitting round the table Rikiki had recently fashioned out of a packing case.

'This is the life,' sighed Donna contentedly as she sat, her eyes shining. She was wonderfully happy; she had never had so much fun or led such an intriguing life before. 'Oh, Rikiki,' she said, 'didn't you mention some sort of plan that you wanted me to help with? Why don't we discuss it over breakfast?'

'Well, it's very simple,' he began rather self-consciously. 'First of all it's essential we avoid being captured by the Boss because of the consequences. I mean Rufus would probably meet a horrible fate as a punishment for daring to escape, and I would probably be held hostage again for the purpose of leading the cat world to its doom. No, this mustn't happen. So I decided the best way to put the Boss off our tails would be to make him think we were dead, and therefore unable to be a nuisance to him.'

'That's a great idea,' breathed Rufus, 'but how on earth . . . ?'

'We'll get Donna to pretend to bury us!' he said with an air that he was aware of announcing something terribly clever. 'She can hold a burial for us in the back garden as though we had suddenly and accidentally died. Then the spy watching the house will run back to the Boss and report what he has seen. Well – what do you think?'

There was a silence for a few seconds while Rufus and Donna thought it over. Then finally they pronounced their judgement. 'Why, it's a marvellous plan! And it should work too.'

'Good,' Rikiki smiled. 'Then we go into action as soon as possible.'

*

In the garden of the deserted house a strange scene was taking place. Beneath a giant oak tree a dark-haired girl was performing a bewildering ceremony. At least it was bewildering to the two spectators in the tree above her. Their eyes widened as she lifted two objects covered in sheets into holes she had made and then covered them with earth. They listened avidly as she said something over them. The words 'Rikiki' and

'Rufus' floated to their ears. A chipmunk, who was one spectator, whispered orders to a mouse, who was the other, when he realized what was happening.

'It's a burial. Slide down the other side of the tree and report to the Boss. Tell him it's the mouse and cat he told us to watch for.'

'Right,' said the mouse, sliding down the tree and running off to obey the chipmunk's orders.

The chipmunk looked down through the leafy branches and thought. He remembered Rufus when he was working for the Boss. Nice quiet little fellow. He'd liked him. Anyway he'd seemed much nicer than some of those other mice in high offices who really seemed to be enjoying their work. He wished that he had been able to escape as Rufus had, but he liked life too much to risk death. All the same, perhaps it was worth thinking about. He hated the Boss and he hated having to spy, just because, like so many others, he had to have money to live. Perhaps he would try to think of a good plan later.

While he was concentrating so hard on all these thoughts, however, he almost fell out of the tree when he saw the most extraordinary sight below him. 'Ghosts!' he exclaimed under his breath. There, standing and laughing with the dark-haired girl, were Rikiki and Rufus. Their conversation floated up to him.

'We saw a mouse running as hard as his legs would carry him in the direction of the backstreet area. Then Rufus recognized him as a spy, and we knew he had taken the bait.'

When the chipmunk heard them talking like that,

with blatant disregard for the code, this time he really did fall out of the tree!

He fell right at their feet and was knocked out by the fall.

The next thing he knew he was in a room filled with the oddest-looking furniture. Three anxious figures were bending over him.

'Are you all right?' asked Rufus.

The chipmunk rubbed his sore head. 'I think so,' he replied, 'but where – oh, I suppose I'm in the old house.'

'That's right,' said Donna, handing him a hot drink, 'now get that down and you'll feel a lot better.'

After he had done so he asked. 'What's going on here?' He pointed to Rikiki and Rufus and added: 'I thought you two were buried. In fact I saw you being buried.'

'No you didn't. What you saw was some stones wrapped artistically in two old sheets. The rest was just presuming, with Donna's help, that it was us,' Rikiki explained.

The chipmunk nodded. 'I think I see.' He turned to Rufus. 'Rufus, do you remember me? I was a spy for the Boss.'

'Yes, I remember you. But what do you mean "was"?'

The chipmunk laughed. 'I resigned,' he said, 'when I fell out of the tree.'

Rikiki gazed at him warily. 'Really?'

'Look,' said the chipmunk, sitting up suddenly, 'I'm serious. I hate the Boss. I was planning to get out of the organization even as I was spying on you. Do you think somehow you can get me out?'

'Do you really mean that?' asked Rikiki.

'Yes, with all my heart.'

'What's your name?'

'Oscar.'

'Hum. This calls for a conference. Do you mind if we go over to that corner and discuss it?'

'Not at all.'

Rikiki, Rufus and Donna huddled together. 'Well, what do you think he's like? You knew him,' Rikiki demanded of Rufus.

'Well, firstly, he's a jolly nice fellow. Always laughing and joking. He never seems to be sad. Of course, I didn't know him terribly well. But if you want my opinion, I think we should help him, he seems sincere. He was always kind to me when I worked with him. And another thing, he seems to have a distinct distaste for the Boss. That's in his favour. Well, that's all I know. What do you think?'

'I say we ought to do as Rufus says,' Donna put in.

'Well, I agree too, so it's an overwhelming majority,' Rikiki said. They all went back to Oscar.

The chipmunk had been watching them anxiously. 'What did you decide?' he questioned.

Rikiki answered: 'You can stay with us if you can think of a good explanation of your disappearance for the Boss. We can't have him snooping around here for obvious reasons.'

'Thank you!' he cried. 'This is what I've wanted for such a long time – I hope I'm not dreaming!'

'I can assure you you're not because we certainly aren't,' said Rufus practically. 'Now what can we do so that you can disappear without any questions being asked? Let's try and think for a few minutes.'

'Right,' they agreed and settled down to do so.

'Well, I think the best plan,' began Oscar, 'would be for me to be reported dead as well. I know it might seem suspicious that I am supposedly killed after having been spying on you but I think it would sound all right if the Boss is made to think it happened a long way from here and for quite an obvious sort of reason.'

'Yes, that's a good idea,' mused Rikiki, 'but we'd have to be very careful how it was done.'

'I know!' Oscar went on. 'Tomorrow I'll write the Boss a much tear-splattered letter and sign it from my sister (though I haven't got a sister, but he won't know that). It will tell of my unfortunate death on the high road miles from here.'

'Good,' said Donna, 'then it's all settled.'

'Well, I feel a lot better now,' said Rufus in relief.

'So do I,' acknowledged Oscar. 'You know this is a nice little hiding place you've got here. None of the spies could spot it. Everyone was pretty sure you'd got away from the house somehow, but the Boss insisted it be watched.'

'Tell us what's been happening, Oscar,' Donna requested in curiosity.

Oscar had been told that Donna knew about the code. He had suspected as much before, but now it was definite he felt more comfortable talking to her.

'Well, a great many things have happened since Rufus went. For one, the Boss managed to capture another cat, for hostage purposes, and war has been declared.'

'How horrible,' said Donna with a shiver. She was beginning to realize what a hard time the inhabitants of Mousetown were having. 'I wish something could be done about it.'

'So does everyone, Donna . . . that is your name, isn't it? May I call you by it?'

'Certainly.'

'As I was saying, so does everyone, except for the Boss and his close friends, but what can they do about it? A full-scale revolution would mean too much loss of life and, besides, no one would dare to lead them. If they go along with the Boss at least there is money for them every week and a much slimmer chance of dying. It might be different now they realize a little more just how evil he actually is, but I doubt it.'

'You know,' said Oscar slowly, 'I'm sure there must be some other way to do something for the mice.'

'You – you mean to overthrow the Boss somehow? Oh, no, Oscar, it's too dangerous, don't even think of it.' Fright was in Rufus's face.

But Rufus was too late. The dawning light of an idea had crept into Rikiki's eyes at Oscar's words. He was always getting ideas and good ones too, so Rufus had reason to say: 'No, Rikiki, don't you dare come up with one of your bright ideas.'

His pleadings were no use. Rikiki began to speak.

'Yes, this is indeed a wonderful hideout. The attic could be used as well – '

Donna was listening, hoping. She prompted him. 'Go on, Rikiki, used for what?'

'Why, the headquarters of course. The headquarters for our own spy ring.'

'Spy ring!'

'Yes. We would win our spies from those already working for the Boss. You two,' Rikiki indicated Rufus and Oscar, 'know a great many discontented mice who are in the Boss's confidence and who would be willing to work for us and let us know his every move. In this way we could make sure that whenever the Boss tried to do anything destructive we would be there before him to keep anyone from being hurt and warning them of his plans before he arrived, Also, at every opportunity we would ruin his weapons, and as much as possible ensure that all the mice who are actually faithful to him are quarrelling among themselves.'

Oscar, becoming even more enthusiastic, added his ideas. 'We could keep a mouse-grocery shop as a "cover" business. Then, when all the spies wanted to report, they would only have to come in, pretend to buy something, say the password to whoever of us is serving and he would be taken – say into the back part of the cellar, which would be curtained off from the shop.'

'Wonderful!' cried Rufus, 'then the Boss would find he wasn't having a war at all, just a game of hide-and-seek.'

'And you *do* know a lot of mice between you who'd be willing to spy, don't you?' said Donna.

'Lots. Come on, Oscar, let's make a list of those we can be sure of, and set about contacting them.'

'Hadn't we better make up a password first?' Donna asked.

'Definitely,' Rikiki broke in. 'It must be something that wouldn't sound too suspicious if it was said in the presence of someone else – if a customer was to over-hear it, for instance. Perhaps it would be safest if we made it sound like the name of some grocery, then we could easily say we had a supply in the back room.'

'And,' added Rufus, 'it would have to be something nobody else would ask for.'

'How about Catty – er – Katting, no – Kattang, yes, something like that. I know! Katonga Flour?' This was Rikiki's suggestion.

'Not "flour",' mused Rufus, 'it doesn't sound right. I like the way you worked in "Cat", though, because it suits our case. Wait on, what about Katonga Soup?'

'Yes, that's just right,' said Rikiki. 'Do we all agree on that then?'

'Yes,' the others chorused, 'we all agree.'

CHAPTER 7

A Pledge is Given

The cellar and just outside the trapdoor to it was a scene of activity. The sounds of hammer-blows, tins being stacked, shelves being put up and animals occasionally falling off makeshift ladders floated on the air.

The girl and the animals had closed off three-quarters of the cellar by putting up a curtain of sacks, and the remaining quarter at the foot of the stairs was where they were putting the grocery shop. Once more the packing cases and Rikiki's and Donna's skill came to their aid. They also used the rather rusty packing-case nails and a shoe of Donna's as a hammer.

It wasn't as hard as it might have been to get food to sell. Mr Longnose, who had lived next door to Rufus, was one of the few mice rich enough and wily enough to outsmart the Boss and make the grocery business pay. When he was told about the animals' (and Donna's) venture, he was only too pleased to supply them with enough food to start off with.

'Everything's going so beautifully,' sighed Donna happily.

Rufus and Oscar looked up sharply from their work. 'Don't start saying that, it's usually bad luck,' Rufus said tensely.

'Oh,' her smile faded for a second, 'I'm sorry but I just felt so good.'

Rikiki looked down from the ladder. 'I'm almost finished,' he said. 'By the way, have we any candles in stock?'

'I think so,' replied Donna, 'but why do you want them?'

'Ooh,' said Rikiki airily, 'I'll tell you later, it's a secret at the moment.'

He climbed down the ladder a little later and asked, 'Well, can I have a couple?'

Donna looked doubtful. 'Well, I don't like digging into the stores – but I guess you can. They're in that yellow box.'

When he had fetched them and gone behind the curtain and up the chute, the others gazed after him in wonder.

'I can't imagine what he's going to do,' said Donna.

Meanwhile Rikiki had reached the top of the chute. He went out of the room into the hallway, the candles under his arm. He was on his way now to the sloping-ceilinged attic.

He came to the wooden steps that led into the attic. Softly he crept up them and pushed open the door at the top.

The room was as dark as though it was night. Cobwebs and a thick layer of dust had made the only window impenetrable to light. But carefully lighting one of the candles he was able to see all the ancient memories that were lying, forgotten, in the strange little place. Chairs were placed round an old oaken table as though invisible people were sitting there.

There was no other furniture but there were stacks of newspapers and several empty bottles.

'Yes,' thought Rikiki, 'it will do. Now if only I can tidy it up without the others coming up and wanting to know what I'm doing before I've finished.'

The first thing he did was to clear the window so that the sunlight streamed in. Everything looked different in the proper light, for it had all seemed so eerie in the flickering beams and shadows caused by the candle.

He worked silently and industriously for about an hour. In that time he threw out piles of papers and dusted for all he was worth at the table and chairs.

At last he thought it looked reasonably tidy and so he decided now to call his friends so they could see the result of his labour.

The others were quite annoyed down at the nearly completed store. Rikiki, who was the most valuable person because he was good at carpentry, had just disappeared for an hour or more. So when the cat appeared at the top of the chute and called to them they were not to be blamed if they were a little cool towards him. And even more when they heard what he had been doing.

The animals climbed up the chute and waited at the top while Donna came round by the door. When she joined them, Rikiki led the way and the others followed.

They had to admit when they saw the attic that he had made a good job of it.

'There's something strange about it,' said Donna,

peering round, 'it's fascinating. I've never seen anywhere like it.'

'I thought you'd like it,' said Rikiki.

'But it doesn't alter the fact that you deserted us,'
added Donna severely.

'It's almost finished, isn't it?' Rikiki asked.

'Yes, but with little thanks to you. And there are two
more shelves to be put up, and another counter top to
be put on. You said you'd do those things later, I remember.'

'All right. I'll do them now.'

'Now? But you haven't told us why you did all
this.'

'Oh, I'll tell you – later. When we've finished the
shop.'

'Rikiki, we came all the way up here for nothing,'
Rufus said crossly.

'Nonsense, of course it wasn't for nothing. We'll
come back later, and perhaps you'll understand.'

They all traipsed back, Rikiki chuckling and the
others wondering at his mysterious attitude.

*

It was growing dark when three animals and a girl
climbed the steps to the attic. They sat down on the
chairs round the table, though Rufus, being so small,
had to sit on the table so that he could see. Rikiki lit
two candles and stood each firmly in an empty bottle.

'I'm going to tell you now,' he said. 'When I was fix-
ing a shelf from the ladder I had an idea. I thought it
would be a good thing if we made ourselves into a
special band and called ourselves by a special name.

Then we could swear to uphold our ideals in a ceremony of some sort.'

'You mean a band to fight against the Boss such as
we were discussing yesterday?' asked Oscar.

'Yes, that's right. I thought how much more – er –
official we would be if we were a definite band and had
a name. Don't you think so?'

'It sounds wonderful,' said Donna.

'Should be great!' cried Oscar.

'Let's do it,' enthused Rufus.

'Well, why don't we have a meeting right now and
decide everything?' Rikiki was pleased at their en-
thusiasm.

'Right!' they agreed.

Rikiki picked up a piece of wood that vaguely resembled a hammer and tapped the table in front of
him. 'The meeting will now come to order,' the cat
said in a very deep voice.

Everyone 'came to order' swiftly and there was a
hushed silence.

'We have several things to decide,' continued Rikiki
in a more normal tone. 'Firstly on a name.'

'That's going to be hard,' Rufus, who wasn't very
good at that sort of thing, complained.

However, he needn't have worried, for it wasn't
long before Oscar jumped up on his chair in excitement. 'I've got a good one,' he said.

'What is it, Oscar?' Rikiki asked eagerly, but a
little disappointed that he had not thought of one himself.

Oscar, calming himself down, told them. 'I think
"The Rebels" ought to be our name. What do you say?'

Everyone showed admiration.

'How did you think of that?' Rufus asked. 'That's just right.'

'Do you like it, Rikiki?' Donna inquired.

Somehow, Donna and the animals seemed to look upon and treat Rikiki as their leader. That is why it

fell to the cat to make the decision as to whether it would do or not. At first he was tempted to express disapproval because he was jealous, but he did see that the idea was a good one. So he said: 'Yes, I do like it. From now on we are the four Rebels.'

The animals and Donna then went on to officially vote Rikiki as captain of the band. Rikiki protested half-heartedly (for he really wanted to be captain) in favour of Rufus, but everyone, particularly Rufus, insisted.

The Siamese cat was very pleased. He stood up on his chair very importantly. 'Thank you,' he said, 'but I must warn you that I haven't had the experience in leading that, say, Rufus has.' He turned to the mouse. 'Perhaps you'll help me, Rufus, if anything goes wrong.'

Rufus, who was very glad indeed that it was Rikiki and not he who had been chosen, for he had had enough of leading, said cheerfully, 'Certainly.'

'Now,' said Rikiki, a little grandly, 'we must pledge ourselves true to the cause. Everyone raise their arms and say this after me.'

In the gloomy light shed by the candles in the dusty old attic the four friends solemnly repeated these words:

'We pledge on our highest honour to do our utmost to hinder the notorious Joe Fingers in the war he has declared on the cats; and, if it is possible, to destroy the empire he has built up if ever we get the chance.'

Not a word was spoken afterwards and nothing broke the spell of determination as one by one they filed out of the room. They had all pledged on their highest honour and in each of their hearts they truly meant it.

PART TWO

Struggle for Freedom

CHAPTER I

'Password, Please'

The Journey Street grocery store was open for business! Rufus adjusted the black moustache he had just glued on and went out behind the serving counter. With satisfaction he viewed the notices that hung on the walls. 'Low price biscuits', 'bargain soaps', 'two cans of tomatoes for the price of one', and many more similar ones.

The reason for the moustache was that he naturally didn't want to be recognized. It was essential that neither he nor Oscar nor Rikiki should be reported back to the Boss as being alive if any of his mice happened to see them. The best way to avoid this, the Rebels had decided, was to wear a disguise of some sort any time they were not in the back room.

Oscar pulled his peaked cap over his eyes and came out of the back room to help Rufus with the serving. It had been agreed that Donna and Rikiki should stay behind the curtain to deal with the spy reports.

The trapdoor squeaked (it had been propped up to allow animals to enter) and they both looked up to see two customers enter. One was a thin, sour-looking mouse and the other had puffy suspicious-looking eyes and was wearing loud clothes of little taste. The thin mouse drifted around looking at the wares, while the puffy-eyed mouse merely leant against the steps and looked as though he was waiting for something.

Oscar followed the thin mouse who had become lost among the stacks of cans at the further end of the shop. When he found him he asked politely, 'Is there anything I can do for you, sir?'

The thin mouse jumped, turned round and looked at him sourly. He didn't speak for a moment, during which time Oscar twisted his paws nervously. 'You can tell me why,' he said, 'you are selling these goods at such preposterously low prices.'

Oscar goggled with surprise. A lump of fright rose in his throat. He recognized the mouse with a shock.

It was one of the Boss's henchmen by the name of Malvern. He hadn't known him very well, so he hoped he wouldn't see through his disguise.

'Er . . .' he said, thinking desperately, but before he had time to answer, Malvern interrupted in a sinister, threatening voice:

'I have a message for you from Joe Fingers. If you want to stay in business you are to sell your goods at much higher prices. I will come round every week to collect your "contribution" to the Boss's cause, which every shopkeeper must pay. This "contribution" will be made up of any profits this shop makes.'

This was all the mouse said before he strode out of the shop leaving Oscar relieved. Not only had his disguise been a success, but the Rebels had no reason to fear the threats of the Boss against the business, for they had the support of Mr Longnose behind them.

Oscar raced back to the counter and told Rufus in a low voice what had happened.

'Malvern?' he whispered back. 'Why, of course, I thought he looked familiar. But I was more suspicious of the other mouse. I'm almost sure I know him. Anyway, it's my turn to do something now. I'll deal with him.'

'Okay,' said Oscar.

Rufus walked over nervously. Suppose the mouse saw through his different clothes and moustache, and reported him to the Boss!

'Y-you wanted something?' he stuttered.

The mouse looked round furtively. Then, as if satisfied by something, answered: 'Yes. My aunt is ill, and asked specially for some Katonga soup. She understands this is the only place where she can get it. Would it be too much trouble?'

Rufus's mouth flew open in surprise. 'Won't you come this way?' he asked quickly. 'I think we have some in the back room.'

The first spy for their side! It had all begun now, thought Rufus. They would have to work hard if they wanted to keep up their ideals. He was proud that it had been he who talked to the spy first.

Reaching the counter he stopped and told Oscar.

'You mean . . .?' Oscar spluttered.

'Yes.' Rufus parted the curtains that divided the cellar, and they all went in. Rufus directed the spy to a chair.

Rikiki asked the question they had prepared to guard against the possibility of the Boss finding out the password. 'What is the colour of the soup?'

'The colour of the blood being shed for freedom.'

'Good,' said Rikiki, any doubt now erased from his mind. This was indeed their first spy. 'Have you any special information?' he inquired.

'I have,' stated the spy as he removed his shock of false hair, pulled off his long false nose and wiped away the make-up that had made his eyes look puffy.

Suddenly Rufus and Oscar recognized him. 'Fergus!' they exclaimed in chorus. When they had made out the list of reliable spies Fergus's name had been among them, but as they had all been strictly ordered to come in disguise they had not known who it was till he removed it in the back room.

Rikiki looked down his list. 'Fergus Wolftwinkle?'

'Yes, that's my name. I have some important information for you.'

'What is it?' Rikiki leant forward in excitement.

Fergus looked nervously towards Donna.

'Don't worry about her. She's taken the promise.'

'Well,' Fergus started, 'the Boss has made his plans for the first raid of the war. It's going to be the Ramon warehouse, the chief living area of the waterside cats. Now this is how it's going to be done.' And in crisp, concise detail he told them all about it.

When he had finished their faces were all grim. Then to the others' surprise a smile spread over Rikiki's face.

'I think I know how to deal with this,' he said.

'How?' they all asked together.

'Well, first of all I must have a volunteer. It will be very dangerous. It can't be you, Rufus, because you're a mouse. But then Donna can't do it either because she's a human.'

'I guess that leaves me then,' said Oscar cheerfully.

'You don't have to if you don't want to, Oscar. I can always do it,' Rikiki said.

'No fear. Just tell me what to do and I'll do it with pleasure.'

'Perhaps,' put in Fergus, 'it would be best if I didn't know your plans. What I don't know can't be forced from me.'

Rikiki looked admiringly at the spy. 'Good thinking,' he praised.

So Fergus left quickly and silently.

'Now,' said Oscar, pulling his chair closer to Rikiki's. 'Explain what I have to do, please.'

'All right,' said the cat, 'your job will be very important. I have already informed the cats of our existence as the Rebels, so at least if you get through with my letter they will know who you are.'

'I gather I am to take them some sort of letter then?'

'You gather right. The letter will contain what Fergus has just been telling us. Upon you will depend the success of our first blow against the Boss. You must deliver this letter to the address by midday tomorrow. Do you understand?'

'I think so.' Oscar's brow creased into a frown of concentration. Rufus at that moment caught a glimpse of the more serious Oscar.

'I wouldn't like to be in his shoes,' thought the mouse. 'No indeed, it would be a terrible responsibility.'

Oscar, though, itched for the next day to come. He was glad he was going to do it. He would show the Boss, he thought, if it was the last thing he did.

Oscar in Action

Oscar waved good-bye to his friends standing by the trapdoor till at last they faded out of sight. Soberly he walked on along Journey Street. He pulled a piece of paper with a few words on it out of his pocket and glanced at it to refresh his memory. It was the address. The address he was going to now.

He was disguised. On his head sat a distinguished black hat, and a thin black moustache perched on his upper lip. A pair of wire-rimmed glasses pinched his nose and he was wearing unobtrusive clothes.

He remembered the good-byes from his friends before he had set off. Rikiki had given him one last chance for them to exchange places, but Oscar had refused.

Putting the paper back in his pocket, he muttered the words on it over and over again under his breath:

'Warehouse 3, Warehouse 3,
Quay Street, Quay Street,
Mousetown, Mousetown.'

This was one time for the usually cheerful Oscar to be serious, deadly serious. He was nearing the waterside area, the immediate neighbour to the backstreet part of Mousetown. It was here that the cats gathered in their greatest force. These cats were not the sort that Rikiki had been, fed every day by an indulgent owner. They were alley cats, who cared for nothing else but the day-to-day business of staying alive. These cats had their own society and kept themselves going by scrounging as much as they could from human workers on the docks. But they were well aware of the happenings in other animal societies besides their own. They knew of the troubles that were going on in the mouse world that extended about their feet. They knew of the war that the Boss was starting against them. Not only had they sent an angry note of warning to the Boss when he captured a second cat hostage, but they were warned of the evil mouse's every move by the spies working secretly for the Rebels. What they were waiting for now was the details of the time and place of the attack which would begin the war.

Finally Oscar reached his destination. He gave the signal knock that had been arranged, on the side door of the warehouse. Three quick and one slow.

A cat opened the door and led him in.

The inside of the warehouse was very large. But far above him every ledge and cranny, and the loft as well, was occupied, not to mention the sea of cats sitting on human-size boxes all around him.

'Password!' demanded a yellow cat, who had one black ear, and who seemed to be the leader, because there was an immediate silence when he spoke.

'Katonga Soup,' Oscar replied carefully.

'What is the colour?'

'The colour of the blood being shed for freedom.'

'Good. Sit down, won't you?' The yellow cat indicated the only empty place Oscar could see in the whole warehouse. Oscar sat down, and every cat's pair of eyes was upon him. 'What news?' he was asked.

Oscar brought forth a piece of paper from his waistcoat.

The yellow cat read it aloud:

'The Boss plans to destroy your warehouse by fire at six o'clock tonight. The mice will attempt to start the fire by lighting oil drums at the back of the warehouse. My advice is to remove all possessions from the inside and make sure no one is trapped. This will make sure that if you fail to stop the mice before they have started the fire, the Boss will have gained nothing. A warning. The Boss is clever and extremely dangerous. Do not underestimate him.

Captain of the Rebels'

There was a subdued silence when he had finished. 'Well, you all heard that,' the yellow cat said impatiently. 'It's all clear enough. Get to work now and see that you are ready in time.'

Amid the sudden bustle and noise of the all at once amazingly active cats, Oscar said to the yellow cat: 'I think I'll stay and see what happens. Perhaps you could spare one of your men to go and tell Rikiki I reached you, and that I am waiting here for a while?'

'Okay,' he was answered, and it was all arranged.

A quarter past five came and went. Half past five. A quarter to six. Six o'clock! The time had come!

'There they are!' one of the cats whispered. 'Over there in those shadows near the back of the warehouse.'

The cats climbed from their hiding places. They

crept stealthily, themselves in the shadows, towards the group of mice.

Oscar was waiting back beside the yellow cat. 'I can't see a sign of the Boss,' he said quietly. 'Blow! I suppose he didn't come, the slimy rascal. I think I'll scout round the front while you are all busy.' He added, 'I mustn't be recognized.'

The yellow cat agreed and then ordered his cats to move forward.

All was quiet at the front of the warehouse. It was almost dark. Oscar looked round to see if he could catch sight of the Boss, just in case, but he had no luck. He heard the sound of the surprise attack as it broke on the air and he smiled.

But he didn't smile for long. Suddenly he felt the smooth cold touch of a revolver in his back.

'Well, well, what a pleasant surprise! Fancy meeting the jolly Oscar here!' The harsh voice that could only

belong to the Boss's second-in-command came to his ears.

'Charlie!' Oscar gasped, 'what are you doing here?'

'Surely that's obvious? What do you think I'm holding at your back? You thought I'd be caught by your fine friends, didn't you?'

'Now look here, Charlie —'

'Oh no, you don't,' the mouse rasped. 'You're going to come and say hello to an old friend of yours. I'm sure the Boss will be very interested to hear how I caught you, won't he, uh?'

'Yes,' replied Oscar helplessly as Charlie forced him down the road, towards the backstreet area. 'He'll be very interested.'

CHAPTER 3

Strange Happenings

Two days after his capture, Oscar once again descended the stairs leading down from the trapdoor into the cellar. There was much relief, joy and back-patting as he did so, for the others had been almost out of their minds with worry and fear. Through their network of spies they had soon learned what had happened and had almost given up hope of ever seeing Oscar again.

They decided to celebrate right away. Rufus took some of the best food from the grocery store and armed with this and the staple drink of the Rebels, cocoa, they all climbed up to the meeting room.

Rikiki proposed a toast to Oscar and when they had drunk they went on to talk about the chipmunk's adventures.

'How did you escape?' Donna wanted to know.

'Well, after I had refused to tell the Boss anything he had me tied up and put in the attic of one of those waterfront cafés. One of our spies must have found out where I was and managed to persuade a waitress to help me. Anyway, she untied my hands and feet and showed me the way out. I hope the Boss doesn't discover who it was or she will be in serious trouble.'

'Poor girl,' Donna said sympathetically. 'But at any rate we're glad you're back.'

The others agreed and then the conversation shifted to a different subject.

It was at this moment that Rikiki chose to reveal something he had learned from a recent visit of Fergus the spy, and which only Rufus as yet knew about.

'In my opinion,' he began, 'the Boss has made his first really big mistake, and one I think we can take advantage of. If we are successful this will almost certainly lead to his final defeat.'

Everyone was listening to him very intently. 'Go on,' Donna urged as he paused momentarily to take a breath.

'His aim had been to occupy us with supposedly fruitless attempts to rescue Oscar – I don't think he has any idea of the extent and power of our organization – while he bombed not only warehouse three, but warehouses one and two as well.'

The reaction was sufficiently astounded to satisfy Rikiki's sense of the dramatic.

'You mean to say he has enough bombs that are strong enough to do that?'

'He has. One of the scientists working for him found that he could make powerful bombs out of revolver bullets. It means that there won't be enough ammunition for any except the really important mice to be armed with revolvers, but he seems to think his scheme is worth it.'

Rufus began to see the point of Rikiki's joy. It meant that at that moment Joe Fingers and his mice had very few weapons to defend themselves if in some way these bombs were destroyed before he had a chance to use them.

Rikiki went on to outline his plan. 'I have also been informed that it is a simple matter to disarm these bombs. All one has to do is to remove the pin in the top of each bomb and pour a little water into it through the gap left by the pin. They then become quite useless. Now this mission is dangerous, even more so than the warehouse raid. Firstly it means going into the Boss's special territory, namely the factory yard. Secondly there is always the danger that the powder will explode. Well, that's it, what do you say?'

'It does sound terribly dangerous,' frowned Oscar. 'Isn't there any other way?'

'No, there isn't. And because it is so dangerous I will do it myself. I have no right to expose any of you to such peril.'

'But –' protested Oscar and Rufus in chorus.

'No buts. I've made up my mind. Besides, I don't want to be sitting behind a desk all the time giving orders. I want to help actively.'

They could do nothing more. Rikiki had no intention of relenting and nothing the others could do or say would make him change his mind. With a final tap of the hammer the rebel leader dismissed the meeting.

It was a little while later that Oscar decided to go for a walk. Down in the cellar he pulled his disguise box from underneath the bed. It was a firm rule that if they went outside they must be disguised. Otherwise it might mean that the Boss would discover their hideout.

As he got ready he thought of Rikiki. There was no one he admired more. To think that not so long ago

he had been one of those cats Oscar had often seen
walking disdainfully up and down the window-sills
of their glassed-in verandahs. It was amazing. And he
was so brave, too; nowhere could they have found a
better leader.

When he had finished he went out by way of the
shop. He picked up a basket of groceries. His new
'shopper' identity was complete.

He wandered aimlessly round the garden, and finally
sat down on the front fence, looking to any passerby
as though he was just having a rest. He was shaded by
a huge tree as he sat there, the basket at his feet.

He sat for ten minutes. He would have stayed longer
if something had not happened.

There was a sudden noise as a large black car swept
into Journey Street. Oscar turned and stared. In the
front seat the chauffeur, a thin man, held himself
primly. In the back sat a smart-looking old lady who
seemed to be looking at all the numbers of the houses.
Then the car stopped. Outside the old house!

The old lady climbed out. She was wearing a grey-
blue suit and a soft grey-feathered hat. She opened the
gate and paused a moment to tut-tut at the state of the
garden. Then she wound her way up to the front door
and took out a key.

A second later another car roared into Journey
Street. It too stopped outside the old house. A man
got out, looked at the other car and at the house. Then
he saw the lady at the front door, waved to her, and
walked briskly up to join her.

'Ah, madam,' the chipmunk heard him say, 'I see
you arrived before me. Let us go inside.'

When they went inside, Oscar went into action.

Rufus was serving when he rushed in, but the customer was just going out.

Oscar explained excitedly what had happened. Rufus looked very grave. 'I expect Rikiki will agree this calls for an emergency meeting.'

They went through the curtain. Rikiki stood up. 'What's all the noise you're making about?' he asked. 'Haven't I told you not to talk so loudly in the shop?'

'This is important, Rikiki,' said Oscar, and explained what had happened.

Footsteps sounded overhead. They all looked at each other worriedly.

Rikiki frowned. 'Obviously we can't go up to the attic. We'll have to have the meeting here. Would you stand up and give us a report, please, Oscar?' he said.

Though they had heard it before, it was much clearer and much more official to have it told again.

'Now,' Rikiki pulled at his whiskers, 'has anyone any explanation or ideas?'

They all looked blank.

Suddenly Rikiki thumped the box he was sitting on. 'I've got it!'

'What?' everyone chorused.

Rikiki looked at Rufus. 'Do you remember a sign in the garden when we first came here? It was in the middle of a patch of rose bushes. You could hardly see it.'

Rufus thought deeply. 'No,' he said at last, 'I don't.'

'Well, I do. It had ". . R SALE" on it.'

'That explains everything, then,' Donna said. 'This

old lady probably came to look over the house. Perhaps,' she looked horrified, 'she will even buy it.'

'We can't let that happen. It would be disastrous for the Rebels and the grocery shop. Why, we wouldn't even have anywhere to live,' Rufus said in an awful voice.

'We must do something to make her decide not to buy,' the cat said thoughtfully, 'something to make her believe that the house isn't very sound. Say it has rotten stairs or the roof looks as if it is going to cave in. She wouldn't be so keen to buy it then, would she?'

They all agreed it was a good idea.

'All right then. We go into operation right now.'

'How are we going to do it?' asked Donna.

'All lean closer,' said Rikiki, 'and I'll tell you.'

CHAPTER 4

Sold!

Mrs Ross looked round the dusty hallway. Then she climbed the stairs and peeped into the first room at the top of them. She tried to imagine what it would be like if it were clean and freshly painted. She liked what she imagined.

She turned to the estate agent who hovered near her. 'Is there an attic?' she asked. 'I have so many things collected on my travels that I would store there if I bought the house.'

'Yes, of course,' replied the agent, and showed her up the stairs to the door.

'Tell me,' said Mrs Ross, as she looked into the gloomy attic, 'why hasn't this house been sold before?'

This was the question that the agent had been dreading, but he was an honest man and said, 'It is supposed to be haunted.'

'Oh, I see,' murmured Mrs Ross, not really taking in what had been said. 'I doubt that a ghost would bother me. I think the house is delightful and I would like to buy it. When we get back would you be good enough to sign it over to me and prepare the contract, or whatever you have to do, so that I can move in as soon as possible?'

'Oh, yes, madam, certainly madam. You should be

able to move in in a couple of weeks if there are no difficulties. Now have you seen enough?'

'Yes, but I think I'll call my chauffeur up to have a look.' She leaned out of the nearest window (for that was her way of doing things) and did so. 'John,' she cried, 'lock up the car and come and see what you think of the house!'

John had just been dozing happily over the paper that he had pulled out of the glove compartment and didn't take kindly to being awakened. He had been the old lady's chauffeur, however, ever since she had come back from abroad, and he knew she always meant what she said. Muttering grumpily to himself, he put away the paper and locked up the car as he had been instructed.

Striding quickly up the path, he reached the door and shoved it open with his foot. It fell back with an eerie creak.

Five pairs of eyes watched as he mounted the stairs.

The fifth step shifted. The sixth fell away under his feet and John crashed to the bottom with a tremendous yell.

The eyes gleamed.

Mrs Ross looked down, alarmed, from the top. 'Are you all right?' she asked.

John sat up slowly and rubbed his head. 'No I am not!' he barked angrily, 'those stupid stairs are rotten!'

Mrs Ross descended to the place where the sixth stair should have been. 'Fiddlesticks!' she declared, 'these stairs are perfectly firm. Why, from where I am I can see the stair itself is in one piece.' She stepped over the hole and went down to where the stair lay.

She picked it up. 'Why, the nails have been levered out!' she explained. 'What happened to you was no accident.' She looked around. So did John.

'Then that means,' he looked puzzled, 'that someone doesn't want us to have this place. I wonder why?'

'I don't know why, but it hasn't altered my decision.' She turned to the real-estate agent, who had followed her down. 'Mr Biggs, you may consider this charming house sold.'

The eyes looked alarmed, then disappeared.

*

Rufus looked at Rikiki. 'Well, what are we going to do now?' he asked.

Rikiki looked worried. 'I don't know,' he said.

'We can't prevent her from buying the house, can we?' put in Oscar.

'No-o,' Rikiki answered, 'but we can do our best to prevent her from finding us, at least till the war is ended.'

'How?'

'We can ... we can seal up the chute, and – and we can close down the grocery store.'

They all looked horrified. 'Close it down!' they exclaimed, 'but what about all the spies?'

'Now listen to me,' said Rikiki, and there was an immediate silence. 'I don't mean that we stop being the Rebels, I mean that we stop being grocers. Now, when this lady buys the house, that means that she will probably have in workers to do up the house and garden, doesn't it? Well, those workers would be sure to find the grocery shop, they couldn't help it. But if we sealed off both the entrances to the cellar, then they wouldn't even be sure that there was a cellar at all. Am I right?'

'Ye-es,' they acknowledged reluctantly, 'but it's a pity about the shop.'

'I know, but that's what we must do if we want to stay here, and I think we do. Now we had better get to work this minute. Oscar, will you close the chute? That should be easy. Just pull the lever by the window-sill upstairs, then use something to hide the lever. By the way, I discovered that there is a second entrance on the first floor. In the room below. Do the same there. Rufus, Donna and myself will do our best to camouflage the trapdoor. We'll have the news passed around by our spies that our shop has had to close down. Well, I think that's everything. Yes. Now, to work!'

When Oscar had finished he went downstairs and out by the front door. When he arrived at the trapdoor he was amazed at the clever job his friends had done. The vines and creepers on the wall above the trapdoor and the bush beside it had all been used to great advantage. No one would ever have guessed that they hid an entrance to a cellar. He squeezed under the greenery and descended the steps.

'By the way,' Oscar remarked when he saw Rikiki, 'I suppose we will have to live on the stores in the shop.'

'Yes,' the cat replied, 'I don't like it but we have to stay alive.'

'How are we going to tell the spies about this?' Donna wondered.

'I'll tell them on my way to fix the bombs,' Rikiki said.

'Rikiki! You mean to say you're still determined to do this dreadful thing?'

'I am. In fact I intend to go tomorrow. You should be able to hold the fort without any trouble. Just as long as you keep quiet, particularly when the workers are around.'

They looked at him dumbly. It was no use arguing. He seemed determined to commit suicide; all they could do, much as they hated the idea, was to stand by and let him.

*

Rikiki didn't mind. He had to do it. Something was driving him to do it; he didn't know what.

When he set out the next morning it was early. Too early for his friends to be up. He thought as he looked at them, however, that perhaps it was for the best. So he did not say good-bye, he just went, and when they woke he was gone.

*

Donna helped Rufus make the breakfast. Not because she wanted to, but because it was something to do. Oscar was pacing up and down restlessly.

Donna tried to think of something that would cheer them all up, when suddenly she had an idea.

Donna didn't tell them at first. She purposely aroused their curiosity by collecting certain tins from the stock of groceries.

'What are you doing, Donna?' Oscar was unable to contain himself.

She smiled inwardly.

'I'm making soup,' she said.

'You don't usually do the cooking,' stated Rufus. 'Are you giving me a rest?'

'Not exactly,' was her frustrating answer. She began opening tins and mixing powdered milk.

'What kind of soup do you put all those different ingredients in?' Rufus asked.

'The kind I'm making.'

'And what is that?' Rufus countered.

'Katonga Soup,' Donna grinned.

She got the desired reaction. 'Katonga Soup!!! But – '

'I thought it might be rather fun. We could put anything we fancied in, because it is an imaginary soup, and doesn't have a recipe until we give it one.'

Everyone looked enthusiastic.

'Now this is how I thought we might work it,' Donna went on. 'Everyone make out a list of what they would like to put in. Be sensible and don't put sugar or golden syrup in; just vegetables and other things that would make the soup taste nice. Oh, and put lots of red things down because it's supposed to be the colour of blood. Understand? It can be a surprise for Rikiki when he gets back.'

No one said it, but in everyone's mind was the thought 'If he gets back . . .'

This is what Oscar put down:

Can of Tomato Soup	Salt, Pepper
Tomato Sauce	Can of Pea Soup
Asparagus	

Rufus wrote this:

Salt, Pepper	Rice
Cabbage (from garden)	Onions (from garden)
Carrots ,, ,,	

Donna had already decided beforehand, so she did not make a list.

They collected all the ingredients. Oscar fell off a ladder trying to get the tin of asparagus from the top shelf, but he didn't hurt himself.

Donna got out their biggest saucepan (made out of a large can) and they put all their things in it. It looked very queer, but no one minded, though any practical-minded cook would have had a fit, just at the colour.

They cooked it over a sort of fireplace-stove that Rikiki had rigged up, using the chute as a chimney.

Donna peered anxiously into the pot. 'I hope it turns out all right,' she said, 'it looks rather funny.'

At this statement they all had turns looking at it. Oscar couldn't resist dipping his finger in to taste it and received a painful reward for his trouble. Yelling, he dived for the other tub and turned on the cold water.

Rufus, in his serious way, inspected the soup. 'Why, it's halfway between red and purple!' he exclaimed.

'Dark blood,' muttered Oscar, looking again, 'realistic, isn't it?'

They agreed it was. At last it was ready. It was decided that Donna should taste it first, seeing it had been her idea.

Rufus gave her a little in a cup.

They all stood over her, fidgeting, as she tasted it. 'Well?' they cried, 'what is it like?'

She looked up. 'It's delicious,' she said.

*

Rikiki lifted the flask of water and poured a little into the last bomb. He wiped his brow when he had finished and grinned wickedly.

'Well,' he whispered to himself, 'the bombs are useless. Now to getting out of here.'

There was a rustle behind him. Rikiki pricked up his ears in terror. Another rustle. He was sure now. There was only one thing those noises could mean. He was caught on the Boss's special territory. The penalty was to be shot on sight.

'Put your paws up and don't turn round,' came two squeaky voices.

Rikiki was extremely puzzled. 'Why don't they shoot me?' Then he remembered something. What was that Fergus had said about only the very high-up mice having guns now? It was a gamble, but he was going to try to get away, anyway. He was as good as dead if he let them capture him.

Suddenly he was running.

'Come back or we'll shoot,' one mouse yelled. He turned and looked. Neither of the mice had a gun. He went on running and running. Out of the factory territory, out of the backstreet area, till at last he reached Journey Street. Then he stopped to catch his breath.

'That,' he said to himself in a satisfied voice, 'is another mission successfully accomplished.'

CHAPTER 5

The Old Lady

A new black and white painted sign stood among the roses where the old one had been. On it was printed in large letters:

SOLD BY ROBERTSON'S REAL ESTATE

A busy horde of workers swarmed about the lawns, gardens and house. Mrs Ross constantly stood over them, correcting and occasionally arguing. The whole place began to take on a new look. Indignant spiders and protesting birds were turned out of corners and eaves. The roof was re-tiled, glass put into empty window-frames, and carpets laid down, all in the space of a few days. The long-deserted house began to look respectable.

The cellar had not been discovered. The workers had been puzzled not to find an entrance to one, but had concluded that one could not have been built. So the four friends, as yet, had not been found.

They were frightened now on two accounts. One, that the Boss would put two and two together and figure that they were hiding there, or else that the workers would stumble upon them.

They had eaten their fill of the soup. It was indeed delicious. Rikiki liked it especially, which was a good thing because it had really been made for him. In fact it had been such a success that they decided to make some more. Now, three days after the first lot had been concocted, another very large bowl stood cooling in one of the washtubs.

They all flopped down into chairs. They were hot and tired from their exertions.

'Well, that is our food for the next few days,' Rikiki said.

'And we're going to need it too,' Rufus frowned.

They all looked at the mouse anxiously. 'What do you mean, Rufus?' asked Donna.

'Oh, dear. Well, I guess I would have to have told you anyway. The grocery stocks have almost run out. We have to eat, after all, and there are four of us.'

'Well, that's just fine. That's all we needed,' Rikiki said sarcastically.

They all looked gloomy.

'Aha!' Oscar exclaimed.

'Aha what?' Rufus asked crossly.

'Did any of you notice that wheelbarrow outside the trapdoor?'

'Yes. But what are you leading up to?'

'A way to get out of here and over to Mr Longnose for some groceries. All that wheelbarrow has in it is grass. Now if all us animals were to hide under that grass, no one would be any the wiser, would they? Then all we would have to do is wait till someone wheels us across the garden and we would have got out of the cellar without anyone seeing us.'

'Brilliant,' praised Rikiki, 'but what about Donna?'

'Oh, don't worry about me,' Donna said quickly. 'I'll stay here and mind the cellar.'

'All right, then, it's settled,' Rikiki said, and they started up the stairs hurriedly, lest the wheelbarrow be gone when they got up there.

*

When the entrance to the cellar had been closed, and the Rebels more or less forbidden to venture out unless Rikiki gave his permission, Donna had suffered most. She felt cramped and although the cellar was quite large she longed to stretch her legs. No one had been up to the meeting room since Mrs Ross had bought the house and Donna wondered if she had left it as it was. Here was her chance to get some exercise and also some information for the Rebels, even though she hated disobeying Rikiki.

As soon as the animals had gone, she crept up the stone stairs and out into the garden. Quickly she ducked back and waited for a gardener to pass by. When all was clear she crept softly to the front door and into the house.

What a change met her eyes! Although she had been watching the garden being transformed she had not realized that naturally it would be happening to the house too. She felt very guilty as she walked over the newly laid carpets and up the stairs. No one seemed to be about and she reached the attic without trouble.

The room had been completely cleared in preparation for Mrs Ross's furniture. The old meeting place was bare and there was no sign of the things the Rebels had left there.

Donna could not bear it. Although the floor was very dusty, she felt so miserable that she lay down in the dust and cried her heart out.

She was so busy crying that she didn't hear the footsteps on the stairs. Donna did not realize there was anyone else in the room until Mrs Ross spoke.

'My dear, what is the matter?' she asked kindly.

Donna turned round terrified.

Mrs Ross looked at her. The girl had obviously not had a bath in weeks. Her clothes were tattered, and her face pale and hollow. She wondered who on earth this child was, and what she was doing here. 'What is your name, dear?'

'Donna,' she replied, glad the subject had been changed. 'Donna Leyland.'

'Where do you live, Donna?'

The girl looked confused. She didn't know what to say.

'Well, you must live somewhere,' the old lady smiled.

Donna saw there was nothing for it but to tell the truth. This lady wasn't going to let her go now. She might have known she wouldn't be able to go on living with the Rebels for ever. A single tear trickled sadly down her cheek.

'Can I trust you not to tell what I am going to reveal to you?' she asked in a solemn voice.

'Of course.'

Donna told as much of the whole story as she could without revealing the 'Code of Animal-speaking Laws'. Unfortunately, however, she began to speak about the war between the mice and cats. Because she had nothing to back up her story with she herself realized it sounded as though she was making it all up. She grew confused and incoherent.

Mrs Ross believed most of it; but it was clear she doubted the rest. It was probably the shock the girl had undergone after the death of her parents, she thought privately.

The old lady had bought the house after a long world tour. She had only gone on this because she didn't want to be a burden to her newly married daughter. Since she had come back she had been thinking of adopting a child. There had been such a waiting list at all the orphanages, however, that she had given up. Now if some of what Donna told her was true, and if she were willing, well, what could be better than to adopt her?

She put the question to her.

Donna was amazed. 'Adopt me?'

Mrs Ross looked anxious. 'Only if you want me to, of course.'

In a matter-of-fact voice the girl said: 'All right, but have you got a pencil and paper? My friends will be worried to find me gone. I want to leave them a note.'

Mrs Ross thought it best to humour her. 'Here,' she said, and gave her some.

Licking her pencil, Donna asked, 'Where are you going to take me?'

'Well, at the moment I'm staying at a hotel until it's all right for me to move in. I'll take you there and get you some clothes and clean you up a bit.'

Although she pretended to be cool and unmoved by the things that had been taking place in the last few minutes, inside Donna was in a turmoil. She didn't know whether she was doing right in deserting the Rebels, just when they probably needed her; but there was nothing she could do. Besides, she didn't altogether dislike the idea of going with Mrs Ross. If only she had believed her, though; it would have been much easier if she could have told her about the speaking laws, but a promise like that had to be honoured. She started writing.

Dear Rebels,

Please do not think I am purposely deserting you. When you left I went up to the attic. The lady who bought the house found me there. She is very nice but she will not hear of letting me stay. She says she is going to adopt me. I will see you soon, when we move in.

I did not tell her about the speaking laws, and she does

not believe me when I speak about you all and the war. I will be thinking about you a lot.

Love,

Donna

It was time to go. As they went out of the front door, Donna slipped round to the cellar and put the note in the shop.

'Are you ready to go?' came the old lady's voice.

Donna took one last look at the place that had been her home for the last two months. 'Yes,' she said, 'I am.'

CHAPTER 6

The Fate of the Soup

The three remaining rebels arrived back with the food the same way that they had slipped out. They laughed over it as they cautiously climbed out of the wheelbarrow, laden with goods, and, after lifting the trapdoor, hurried down into the shop. Putting his food tins on the shelves, Rikiki called to Donna. To his surprise there was no answer. He called again. Once more no answer. He strode up to the curtain and put his head into the cellar.

'Donna,' he began. He blinked in amazement. There was no sign of her.

'Rikiki,' Oscar shouted.

Rikiki raced back. 'Donna's gone!' he panted.

'I know,' Oscar replied, and showed the cat the note he had found.

'Oh no.' Rikiki sat down abruptly after reading it.

A mist of gloom descended. Wearily they put away the rest of the food.

'Anyway,' said Rufus, brightening, 'we'll see her in a week.'

'We hope,' Oscar said pessimistically.

Rikiki thought it best to change the subject. 'You know,' he commented, 'we have no idea about how the war is going. It's a pity we had to close up the store.

But it doesn't matter now, I have arranged a way for the spies to report to us.'

'How?' they all cried.

'Well, this is how it works. I told Mr Longnose to get in touch with Fergus. Now, Oscar, do you remember that tree you fell out of?'

'As if I could forget!' he answered, rubbing his head.

'Well, at the base of it there is a hole. Fergus or some other spy will leave a note, telling us what is happening.'

'Do you suppose there would be a message there now?' Rufus wondered.

'No, I don't expect it would get there for a few hours yet. We have only just arrived back, after all. We will have to collect it late at night when the Boss's spies are sleeping on the job.'

'How do we know that they'll be sleeping on the job?'

'We don't. We will just have to take the chance. But I think if we are late enough they are pretty sure to be.'

'When exactly will we chance it?'

'Tomorrow, before dawn. Okay? Good. Till dawn then, comrades.' He raised his mug of cocoa that Rufus had prepared.

'Till dawn,' they agreed, and drank.

*

The night was dark. The time was four in the morning. Two of the Boss's spies snored behind a bush, in the corner of the garden. Three strangely garbed animals crept from the cellar.

'Psssst!' Oscar hissed to Rikiki.

'What?'

'How are we going to see to get to the tree?'

'We're not. We can't risk a light. Now be quiet or you'll wake our friends.'

One by one they stumbled across the garden. It was like playing blind without the comfort that you could open your eyes any time you wished. They were dressed in dark clothes and wore masks. If they were seen they would not easily be recognized.

Suddenly Oscar tripped. 'Owwww . . .' his cry trailed off guiltily.

'Oh, Oscar!' Rufus said, 'are you all right?'

Rikiki ground his teeth.

'I think so,' Oscar replied in a small voice.

'Well, you won't be,' Rikiki said softly in a voice edged with ice, 'if we ever get back to the cellar. Now shut up for heaven's sake, and let's go on.'

They listened for a few seconds, and to their relief the snoring continued uninterrupted.

They arrived at the tree. Holding his breath, Rikiki reached inside. His paw closed over a piece of paper.

'Hurray,' they said softly.

They traipsed back. Oscar took care not to trip, and all was well.

They all gasped in relief when they arrived back safely. Oscar looked fearfully at Rikiki, but he made no mention of the incident. He was too busy reading the note.

When he had finished, his mouth dropped open. 'Oh no!' he exclaimed.

Oscar seized the message and read it out.

'Rikiki, urgent.

The Boss has had enough of you and the rebels and he plans to force his way into the cellar with a thousand of his men. I do not know when, but it should be soon. Good luck to you all, you're going to need it.

F.'

They all turned to their leader, the Siamese cat, and as they had done so many times before, asked, 'Well, Rikiki, what are we going to do?'

Rikiki looked blank. 'I haven't the faintest idea. But for the moment we had better set about barricading the trapdoor. By then I will have thought of something. Anyone else's ideas would be very welcome, too.'

Just then Rufus was rewarded with one of his rare but usually good ideas. Rikiki noticed him staring into the air and asked, 'Rufus?'

'If,' the mouse answered, 'we could somehow manage to talk to those mice without the fear that the Boss would punish them for being disloyal, then I'm sure we could persuade them to stop fighting the cats. After all, the Boss can do nothing without an army. I know most of them. They would listen to me. Besides, except for a few like Charlie, they all hate the Boss like poison. I'm sure if they all had a chance to become honest citizens again they would grab it.'

Rikiki looked thoughtful. 'Yes, I think you've got something there, Rufus. We must work along those lines. However, we still have the problem of what to do about the Boss and those who really follow him.'

'We'll think of something,' said Oscar, joining in.

'Well, I hope so,' Rikiki said.

*

Mrs Ross came back the next day to get everything finally ready for when she moved in. It was while she was in the room on the first floor next to the stairs that she noticed something queer. She observed a laundry chute, but nowhere could she find either the entrance or where it ended.

'If I knew there was a cellar I would think it ended there, but – Wait a minute, didn't Donna say she had been living in the cellar? Now that's funny; the workers couldn't find one. Now let me think. Ah, I remember, Donna said the chute led to the cellar all right. But they sealed it up for some reason. Now there I am saying "they" sealed it up. Now how could animals – if there were any at all – oh, it's so confusing. Wait. I know. There was an entrance on this floor.'

She examined the chute. Suddenly she saw how it had been closed. She opened it, and peered down.

She had a view of the whole cellar. It was then she had the shock of her life!

*

A fat, greasy mouse stood, an avenging grin on his face, at the foot of a flight of stone stairs. Behind him were rows and rows, and still more, of mice, ranging to the top of an open trapdoor. About them were the ruins of a barricade; furniture, food tins and other things lay, broken and dented, all over the floor. At the opposite end of the cellar (the shop and cellar were one now, the curtain having been torn down) was a small group of animals. One was a handsome Siamese cat with a leather collar round his neck, another was a plump, bespectacled mouse, and the last was a furry brown chipmunk.

With surprise Mrs Ross recognized them. They were the animals Donna had tearfully described and urged her to believe in. She felt ashamed.

The Boss's voice cut, just as it had on that day when Rufus had been late, like a whiplash across the room.

'You in the brown collar are Rikiki, leader of the Rebels, I presume?'

'You presume correctly,' Rikiki answered quickly.

'I also presume you know why I have come?'

'I do,' Rikiki replied promptly.

'Then,' the Boss said, 'you might be so kind as to oblige me by giving up now, and save the fighting that,' he nodded to his men who stood behind him, 'can only end in disaster for you.'

'We have to refuse your kind offer, I am afraid, Mr Fingers. Now, perhaps you will be good enough to listen to our proposition.'

'But of course.'

'You have a very peculiar skill, have you not, Mr Fingers? Skill that enables you to balance on a small area for a long time?'

'Yes, but why do you ask me that?'

'Because,' broke in Rufus, 'I challenge you to a contest, Joe, the winner of which gives in to the other.'

The Boss stared at him in wonder. Rufus was challenging him! He felt like laughing.

'Aw, go on, Boss,' urged Charlie, 'what have you got to lose? No one has ever beaten you yet, and, besides, it'll be a quick way of getting it all over and done with.'

'True, true,' mused the Boss. 'All right,' he shouted back at last. 'Where do we have this contest?'

With an effort, Rikiki pulled out the bowl that was still half full of Katonga Soup. 'On the edge of this,' he told him.

The Boss looked at it doubtfully. Why, a slip of the foot and he would drown! He didn't like it, but he couldn't back out now. 'Okay,' he agreed.

'Are you sure you want to go through with it?' Rikiki and Oscar asked.

'Yes.' Rufus swallowed.

He started towards the bowl where the Boss waited. But when he had gone only a few steps he turned. Then he did the strangest thing. Making sure no one but the Rebels saw him, he winked solemnly.

'What was that in aid of?' Oscar asked Rikiki, mystified.

Rikiki didn't hear him.

The actual climbing on to the edge of the bowl was included in the contest. The two mice slithered inch by inch, using as footholds the glass pattern.

Rikiki was very angry with himself. Angry for letting Rufus go ahead with his hare-brained scheme. Heaven only knew what would happen now!

The Boss reached the top first. There was a tiny smattering of applause from his more loyal followers. He was so intent on balancing that he didn't dare rebuke the others.

There was a lot more cheering when Rufus got there. A lot of his old friends among the mice clapped and whistled loudly. The Boss frowned like a thundercloud.

They had been balancing about five minutes when it happened. It would have been safe if Rufus hadn't looked down. The very sight of it lying so still so far down made him dizzy.

Rikiki noticed that he was swaying. 'Rufus!' he cried in anguish. But it was too late.

There was a silence and the Boss grinned. He couldn't resist looking down at Rufus. That was his undoing. With a yell that in no way resembled his usual oily speech, he joined his enemy in the thick red soup.

The mice and the Rebels joined in the pushing over of the bowl with the faint hope of rescuing them before they drowned.

Crash! The bowl rolled over and split in half. The first force of the soup pushed them back.

The Boss floated past them, face down. The mice took off their hats.

A small bundle of fur, with a fine example of the Australian crawl, swam up to Rikiki. When he stood up in the now mouse-waist-deep soup, the cat gasped. 'Rufus!'

Everyone crowded round. 'Hurray for Rufus!' they cried. 'Hip hip hurray!'

Oscar asked something that had been bothering him. 'Rufus, why did you wink at us before the contest?'

The mouse laughed heartily. 'That was because you all seemed so worried. I never had any doubts that it wouldn't happen as it did.'

'Why not?'

'I knew the Boss couldn't swim.'

*

'Well!' exclaimed Mrs Ross, getting out of her cramped position. 'I see now. It was all true! I shall have to hurry back as fast as I can and apologize to Donna.'

CHAPTER 7

One Last Look

Rikiki tapped his hammer loudly on the table and brought the meeting of the Rebels to order. They were all sitting round the table in the old attic. The chattering ceased abruptly and they turned their eyes upon the Siamese cat.

He stood up. 'We are very pleased,' he began importantly, 'to have Donna with us after a week's absence. She – '

'Don't forget to say that I'm here for always now,' prompted the girl herself.

'Sssh!' rebuked Rikiki, 'you're interrupting my speech. I have all this to say yet.' He brought out a huge wad of papers.

'Oh no,' they all groaned.

The cat laughed. When he recovered he reassured them. 'Oh don't worry, I have no intention of burdening you with this. However, we have got a lot of things to talk about. The first is the most serious.' He took a deep breath. 'And that is the disbanding of the Rebels.'

Everyone looked horrified. Agitated discussion broke out. Rikiki tapped his hammer again to quieten them.

'Listen to me,' he said. 'The Rebels have done their

job. I don't mean that we can't reband again if trouble arises, but it was only formed in the first place to destroy the empire that Joe Fingers set up. Do you remember when we made that pledge?'

'It seems such a long time ago, doesn't it?' Rufus reflected. 'So much has happened since then.'

'Well,' Oscar said, 'I agree with Rikiki. I don't want to disband at all, but I think it would be for the best.'

'Let's take a vote on it,' Donna suggested.

'Right,' agreed Rikiki; 'all those in favour of disbanding say "aye".'

'Aye!' came the solemn chorus of voices.

'Good,' said Rikiki, 'I'm glad you all agree. I wouldn't have liked it at all otherwise.'

'But don't let's do it before the end of the meeting,' pleaded Rufus, 'I think we'd all feel better that way.'

Rikiki nodded his head. 'Now before I get on with something else, has anyone anything that they would like to say?'

'Yes, I have.' Donna rose from her seat. 'Aunt Amanda, that is you know her as Mrs Ross, told me to ask you if you would like to live here for ever.'

'Here?'

'She wants you all to stay. She – she found out about the "Code of Speaking Laws". She saw you speaking and I had to tell her all about it after that; but I made her take the promise, of course. I didn't ask her about letting you stay, either, she suggested it. Oh, Rebels,' Donna asked excitedly, 'isn't it wonderful?'

They all stared at her, wide-eyed. 'Wonderful?'

Rikiki queried, 'it's absolutely magnificently marvellous!'

'Oh, Rikiki!' they laughed.

'I suggest we give Donna's Aunt Amanda three hearty cheers.'

And they did.

'Now has anyone else anything to say?' Rikiki looked round. 'No? Well, now I can tell you, or, rather, show you, something pleasant too.' The cat picked up the brown-paper parcel from beside his chair and began to unwrap it. The parcel had caused a lot of speculation when he had brought it into the room.

One by one the layers came off. Finally Rikiki held up what looked like a piece of wood. When they looked closer, however, they saw that it was a plaque with some sort of writing on it.

They leaned closer to read it.

This plaque is presented to the Rebels as a small token of thanks from the mice and the cats. Without your valued help many of us would not be alive today. May you all be blessed.

'Now that was very nice of them,' remarked Rufus thoughtfully. 'It makes it all seem worth while, doesn't it?'

Rufus suddenly remembered something he had to tell them. 'I was out on the lawn watching the workers yesterday,' he remarked. 'They were trimming the ivy off the walls of the house. Then – well, have you ever wondered whether this house had a name?'

'Often,' said Donna.

This plaque
is presented to
The Rebels
as a small to
thanks from
the cats. You
many of us
May you al be fe

'Well,' Rufus continued, 'when they cut away the ivy just above the front door they found a brass plate with a name on it.'

'What was it?'

'Journey's End.'

'How lovely!' exclaimed Donna.

'It does seem appropriate, doesn't it?' agreed Rufus.

After a little while Rikiki stood up, looking very serious. 'Is there anything else we have to talk about?' he asked.

'Oh, Rikiki! We're – not – ' cried Donna.

'I'm afraid it must be,' Rikiki said sadly.

'Well,' said Oscar defiantly, 'if we must do it, it might as well be in style. Why don't we re-create the time when we made the pledge? I mean, get some candles and put something over the windows and make it dark – '

'Yes, why don't we?' enthused Donna. 'I would like it very much.'

'Well, okay,' said Rikiki. 'Where are the candles?'

'In the cellar,' Donna answered. 'I'll go and get them.'

As Donna sped away, Rikiki and Oscar set about putting up some sort of curtain. The room was soon cloaked in darkness.

'Where has that girl got to?' grumbled Rikiki when they had sat in the darkness for a while.

Eventually two points of light appeared and everyone could see. 'I had trouble lighting them,' Donna explained.

'Are we all in a circle round the table?' Rikiki asked in a deep voice.

'Yes,' they chorused in answer.

'Good. Now repeat after me. "We hereby dissolve the pledge we made exactly two months and three days ago. We dissolve it only because we have fulfilled it. One week ago the notorious Joe Fingers was killed, and therefore his empire destroyed. May the freedom gained ever live on."'

They were perfectly quiet for a moment.

Rikiki sighed. 'It's done,' he said at last. 'We are no longer the Rebels.'

'What about some cocoa, Rufus?' Oscar inquired.

'Sure,' said Rufus. 'Actually I anticipated that.' The mouse jumped down from the table, ran outside and returned toting a huge flask. 'Mrs Ross,' he explained.

'Has it got milk in it, then?' Oscar asked.

'No. I told her to make it the way we've been having it. It seemed right that we should have it our way at the last meeting.'

'Good.' Oscar was pleased. 'I propose a toast to Rikiki, our leader, once captain of the Rebels, who led us to success.'

'Thank you,' Rikiki acknowledged, when Donna and the animals had drunk. 'And I want to propose one back to all of you who helped me.'

Then Rikiki looked at Rufus. 'And we all must thank you, Rufus, for being brave enough to carry out the plan when the Boss invaded the cellar. If it hadn't been for you we wouldn't be here celebrating now. A toast to Rufus, Rebels!'

But Rufus didn't hear them. He was gazing out of the window, a dreamy look on his serious little face; the cheers and clapping of that day were still ringing in his ears.

About the Author

Diana Frances Bell was born in New Zealand but her parents moved to Australia when she was only seven and she has lived in Sydney ever since. At the age of twelve she wrote the first chapter of *The Rebels of Journey's End* as a separate story, put it aside, and forgot it. Some months later she came across it and decided to make it the basis of a full-length book, completing it a few days before her fourteenth birthday. She is interested in acting, is a keen swimmer, and enjoys sailing in Sydney Harbour.

*If you have enjoyed this book and would like to
know about others which we publish, why not join
the Puffin Club? Membership costs 5s. a year for
readers living in the U.K. or the Republic of Ireland,
(15s. in European countries, 25s. elsewhere) and
for this you will be sent the Club magazine* **Puffin Post**
*four times a year and a smart badge and membership
card. You will also be able to enter all the
competitions. There is an application form overleaf.*

Application for membership of the Puffin Club

(Write clearly in block letters)

To: The Puffin Club Secretary,
Penguin Books Ltd,
Harmondsworth, Middlesex

I would like to join the Puffin Club. I enclose my membership fee for one year (see below) and would be glad if you would send me my badge and copy of *Puffin Post*.

Surname ....

Christian name(s) ....

Full Address ....

....

....

Age............... Date of Birth..............................

School (name and address)....................................

....

Where I buy my Puffins.......................................

Signature (optional) .... Date ....

Note: Membership fees for readers living in:
The U.K. or the Republic of Ireland   5s
European countries   15s
Elsewhere   25s